Only for the Holidays

Seasons of Seaside
Book 3

Shannon O'Connor

Only for the Holidays

SEASONS OF SEASIDE #3

SHANNON O'CONNOR

Copyright © 2023 Shannon O'Connor
All rights reserved.

All rights reserved. No part of this publication may be reproduced, distributed, or transmitted in any form or by any means, except in the case of brief quotations embodied in critical reviews and articles.

Any resemblance to persons alive or dead is purely coincidental.

Cover by Blue Moon Creative Studio.

Edited by Victoria Ellis of *Cruel Ink Editing & Design*.

Proofread by Beth Hale of *Magnolia Author Services*.

Formatted by Shannon O'Connor.

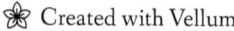 Created with Vellum

Only for the Holidays Playlist

I Belong in your Arms - Chairlift

Sunroof - Nicky Youre & dazy

Crashing (feat. Bahari) - Illenium

As It Was - Harry Styles

Love of My Life - Harry Styles

Santa, Can't You Hear Me -Live - Ariana Grande, Kelly Clarkson

Have Yourself a Merry Little Christmas- Sam Smith

All I Want for Christmas is You - Mariah Carey

Chapter 1

Lynn

I stuff my face full of Christmas tree-shaped Pillsbury cookie dough. It's the inferior shape, really. The Santa Claus ones are so much better, but of course the store was sold out of them. I eat it raw. If you cook it and have your life together that much, I applaud you. But that sure as hell isn't me.

I'm lying on my couch, covered in three winter blankets and a pair of warm, fuzzy socks. No one told me that feet get unreasonably cold as you age. I feel like a freaking newborn with how thick these socks are. But they keep me warm so I don't complain...that much. *The Bachelorette* reruns serve as background noise as I enjoy my day off. I really wish there were an all gay version of this show.

My phone rings, and I sigh as I realize it's my mother. I could ignore it but I know that'll only guarantee more calls.

"Hello?" I answer.

"Finally! Sweetheart, we're trying to plan Christmas, and we were wondering when you're coming this year." This is how she is, no *hello*, no *how's work*, just right to the point of her phone call. I guess I should be thankful.

"Oh, um..." I hesitate. I've been avoiding this call for a week now. The last thing I want is to go home for Christmas. Filled with relatives asking when I'm getting married or having kids even though the only thing I'm committed to is this couch.

"Well, I actually have to work this year," I say. It's a lie. I know she's going to see right through my lie, but I lie anyway and hope for the best.

"You're a *tattoo artist,* surely your boss can spare you for one day?" She says *tattoo artist* in the same tone someone would say *garbage man*. Like it's a looked down upon career and not anything impressive—you know, like my sister being a nurse.

"They can't." I've already lied. I'm committed now.

"Well, it would be nice to see family for the holidays. Especially since you aren't seeing anyone. *Again.* I don't want you to get too lonely up there." There it is, the judgmental tone and the snide comment about how I'll be alone for the holidays. Even though this is the way I like it, no one can fathom someone enjoying spending time on their own.

"I'm not going to be alone," I say, about to mention Furball, my cat.

"Your cat doesn't count, dear." She sighs.

"I'm actually going to be staying here so I can meet my girlfriend's family." The lie slips out even easier than the last one.

"What?!" My mother isn't shocked because I'm gay. She's known that for the last fifteen years, but the fact that I could possibly be seeing someone? That's what's shocked her.

"It's nothing serious yet, but she wants me to meet them. I'm staying home for her." The lie expands. Honestly, if they keep my mother off my back, it's fine by me.

"Oh! Well that's fantastic then! I'm so happy for you."

"Thanks, well I better go. She's actually here, and I don't want to be rude." I lie through my teeth again.

"Of course! Tell her I say hello. Oh, I can't wait to tell your father; he'll be so *relieved* you're not alone again this year."

"Yup, no need to worry about me this year." *Why hadn't I thought of this lie years ago? How many holidays could I have gotten away with pretending to have a girlfriend and really telling some white lies?*

We hang up, and I go back to watching *The Bachelorette* and eating my cookie dough. Surely a few little white lies won't hurt anything, I mean, look at how happy it made my mother. Now I don't have to go home for the holidays, and she'll be off my back from now until at least Valentine's Day. She might eventually ask for details but those can't be hard to come up with if needed. I might actually get away with this.

"Come here, Furball." I call my cat over, and she purrs and climbs on my legs. At least I can count on her. It counts for more than my mother said it did. Cats are great companions, and besides, I only have one. It isn't like I'm some kind of crazy cat lady.

Furball purrs under my touch, and I smile as I pet her. "We can make this holiday season fun, right?" I ask, and she doesn't answer— I don't expect her to.

Chapter 2

Sophie

"Oh, yeah! Oh, hell yeah!" My boyfriend, Kyle thrusts inside me, having the time of his life. I lie here, feeling close to nothing as I think about the dance moves I should be practicing for class tomorrow morning.

"Oh, yeah," I add, unenthusiastically. I can't help it. It's been three months of shitty sex. I feel more like a pocket pussy than a girlfriend, and I'm done faking orgasms for him.

I push Kyle off me, and he grunts, looking at me with wide eyes and an annoyed expression.

"What the hell?! I was so close." He grabs his dick and starts jerking himself off.

"Well, I wasn't." I sigh.

"It's not my fault it takes forever for you to come." He scoffs. I can't remember what the hell I ever saw in him in the first place. Maybe it was the Justin Bieber hair that reminded me of my youth or the abs that he works on daily. I don't care anymore; it's no longer doing anything for me.

"It doesn't take me forever when I'm alone," I retort.

"Whatever. Let me finish on your tits at least." He tugs on his dick and moves closer to me as I move farther away.

"No. I'm done," I say.

"What a fucking cock tease," he says, letting go of his dick.

"I don't mean with *this*. I mean with *us*," I say firmly. I've been thinking about it for a few days now, and it's just becoming more and more obvious the more time I spent with him.

"What? You can't be fucking serious." He shakes his head, moving his blond hair out of his eyes.

"I'm very serious." I stand and grab my leggings and crop top, yanking them on hastily. He doesn't need to see me naked any longer. That's a privilege he doesn't have anymore.

"You're such a fucking bitch. I was going to end this anyway," he spits out.

"Yeah, sure you were." I roll my eyes and pick up my phone.

"Whatever," he grumbles and starts getting dressed. "I can do better; let's see you get anyone who can put up with your moodiness." We head toward the door. I can't get him out of here soon enough.

"Goodbye, Kyle." I wave him off and shut the door behind him. He grumbles something under his breath, but I ignore him.

Once he's out of sight, I take a deep breath and watch out the window until I see him get in his car. I want to head over to the dance studio, but the last thing I want is to run into him in the parking lot. He seems like the type to hang around, and I'm not in the mood for anything else from him.

Thankfully, he peels out of the parking lot in his shitty car. After I finish cleaning myself up, I head down the few flights of stairs and to my car. I dial my best friend Delilah, but she doesn't pick up. Not that I blame her, she's either busy with her fiancé or preparing for the arrival of my godchildren. I'll have to update her about my breakup later.

I decide to head to the dance studio instead of staying home. It's Sunday night, so classes are done for the day. Delilah isn't here, and I'll be able to have the place to myself—which is exactly what I need.

Once I park at Moore Moves, I jump out and lock my car. After using my keys to unlock the front door, I quickly shut off the code to the alarm system and turn on the lights in the studio. It's probably not the safest idea—being here—especially after what happened to the owner of the Cinnamon Roll Saviors. But I'm also trained in self-defense, and I'm more than aware of my surroundings. I lock the door to the studio, just in case, and blast my music. The new Olivia Rodrigo album will do for this. A catchy song blares through the speakers, and I start to dance around.

First, I'm just warming up and moving around as much as I can. Then, I start doing more purposeful moves. I close my eyes and let everything sink from my body. All the feelings I had for Kyle, good and bad, are slipping from my fingertips with each move. I feel the lyrics in my bones, and I sing along—off-key. I just want to feel everything and nothing at once.

I scream the words along to the breakup songs that play, and I realize I've been over Kyle for longer than I realized. Maybe it just actually happened, but in my mind it's been over for a while. I certainly don't feel heartbroken. Honestly...I'm already looking forward to whoever I end up with next. I mean, is it bad that I'm already thinking about putting my Tinder profile back up?

Probably.

. . .

But if you had to fake orgasms for as long as I did, you'd understand.

Dancing around the room, I change the songs, skipping over the slower, sad songs. I decide to choreograph a number for a class I'm teaching. One of the songs on this album is *so* perfect for my class, so I decide to plan out a few steps. I know I'm off the clock, but for someone like me, I'm never *really* off the clock. I can't help it. Dancing is in my bones.

It's actually what first bonded Delilah and me.

We met in college, both of us taking a dance class that partnered us up. It lead to a few midnights where we got to know each other over pirouettes and iced coffees, and we've been inseparable ever since.

I ended up completing a marketing degree, and I run a profitable TikTok account now. Speaking of which, I'm probably due to post a new dance this week. I haven't posted anything in a few days, and I don't want the algorithm to punish me for it. It's a bit of a pain in the ass, but it's also a nice source of income that I don't mind. I go live a few times a week, dancing and talking about dance classes. I also make videos of the trending dances, and even choreograph some of my own. Once in a while my choreo trends, too, which leads to an increase in followers and a bit of a pay raise.

I decide to go *live* and update my followers on my life. I'll show them a new dance eventually, too, but I need to get the hard part out of the way first. I have about 700 followers join, and they all send sad and angry emojis about my breakup. I get it. My followers are invested in my life. Honestly, though, I'm here to dance, and that's all I want to do.

After the update, I set my phone on the ledge Delilah and I built. It gives a perfect angle of the studio. Once I'm positive everything looks good, I start dancing. I start with easy moves that anyone can learn. After showing the viewers the entire dance, I slow it down and go through it a couple more times. I stop to look at the comments, and they love it. I smile. It's so much easier when I'm here. It's a lot less pressure and lower stress. I don't have to fake anything or be anyone I'm not; I can just dance and be myself.

I do the dance a few more times before signing off, and then I do it three times for a video. First fast, second slow, and then a medium speed the last time to give everyone a chance to learn it at their own speed. I upload it since it's a good time according to the algorithm gods, and then I shut off my phone. I'm not calling it a day with dancing, but I needed to call it a day with being on video.

I let out a deep sigh and relax a bit now that I don't have to force a smile. The one thing I hate about going live is the nonstop smiling. At least now I can relax and go back to dancing for myself. I spin around the room on my toes and do a mix of several dances that I love. I don't think about it, I just move.

Chapter 3

Lynn

"Good morning, Addison." I smile as I walk into Rainy Day Tattoos. Addison is our receptionist and fellow artist. We really need to hire a new receptionist but that isn't for me to say or do. I just know Addison wants to focus more on tattooing these days.

"Good morning, Lynn." She smiles back. Her blonde hair is tied back in a tight bun today, and her son, Aaron, isn't with her. He's either at school or with Addison's wife, Nova. They tied the knot a few months ago, and even though they hid it at first, they eventually came clean about it. I'm just happy for Addison to have someone.

"Any new appointments?" I ask as I set down my stuff in my area.

"One. It's a walk in, but you'll want to take her. She wants a Medusa tattoo," she quietly says.

"Got it. Give me a moment to get set up, and I'll be ready."

I agreed on a policy with Reagan, the owner of the studio, when I started; anyone who comes in requesting a Medusa tattoo gets it for free—no questions asked. I know the meaning behind the Medusa tattoo all too well. I have one on my right shoulder. It's commonly known as a survivor tattoo, and people get it after being sexually assaulted as a tattoo that signifies empowerment. More often than not, the client ends up talking about their experience, and it's a bit of word vomit that I don't mind. Tattoos are healing, and I want to help in any way that I can. I give them a card for a local therapist when I'm finished with their piece and send them on their way, hoping that the tattoo gives them just a little bit of their power back.

"Hi, I'm Lynn," I introduce myself to the woman waiting at the front of the shop. She's timid and has small features, but she lights up when she sees me.

"Hi, I'm Kate. I follow you on Instagram, and I've admired what you've been doing for others with the Medusa tattoos. I was looking to get one, and I just wanted to tell you how cool it is that you've been doing this for free." She gushes at me.

"It's the least I can do," I say with a shrug. It's no skin off my back. Sure, it's a few hours of unpaid work, but it's for a good cause.

"Well, it's certainly appreciated." She smiles.

"Do you have an idea of the type of Medusa you want?" I ask, bringing her into my room.

"Yes." She nods and takes out her phone. She pulls up a picture of a tarot card Medusa. I've seen a few of these done before but I've never done one myself. It isn't outside of my capabilities, though.

"This is beautiful." I smile and take her phone from her. "Can I send this to myself to print?"

"Of course." She hands me the phone and takes a seat on the table.

"I'll be right back." I send myself the photo and head to the printer.

Only for the Holidays

Once I grab my iPad and the printed photo, I return to my space and take a seat across from Kate.

"So, I'm going to draw this in my style. It's going to look a little different but it'll have the same elements. If you're familiar with my Instagram you shouldn't have a problem with how it comes out. But we can change anything you don't like. I want this tattoo to be something you 100% want and love," I explain. "That's the most important aspect of all of this."

"I'm sure I'm going to love it." She smiles.

"I'm a great listener if you feel like you want to talk about anything during your tattoo, but if not, I understand. Just let me know where you stand."

"I think I'd like to keep the story to myself. Well, my therapist knows, too, but I'm okay. She suggested I come here, actually. Thought it might be a good step in my healing process," she explains.

"I love that. We stan a supportive therapist." I chuckle lightly.

"She's the best. I don't know what I'd do without her," she says, laughing nervously.

"We've all been there." I slide over and show Kate my own Medusa tattoo. She takes a deep breath, and I see her shoulders relax.

"Oh, thank goodness." Her eyes widen. "Not thank goodness. That came out wrong. It's just comforting that I'm not alone in my trauma." She pauses and shakes her head. "Oh my gosh, what am I thinking? I just meant—"

"No worries. I know what you mean. It's good to know you're not alone in this." I go to place a hand on her shoulder but I stop myself. The last thing I'd want is someone I don't know touching me so intimately.

"Yes, exactly. It's not like I talk to my friends about stuff like this." She sighs.

11

"I'm sure they'd understand and want to be there for you if you gave them the chance." I smile. Even though I'm a total hypocrite.

I had slapped a tattoo on my trauma and never looked back. Sure, I do my part in therapy but that doesn't magically fix everything. There's a reason I haven't brought anyone home in so long. Not that my parents would understand that or even have any idea. They think my tattoos are just art, and I haven't done much to make them think otherwise.

After finishing up the drawing of the tarot card, I show it to Kate and she squeals happily. "I love it!"

"Perfect, let me get the ink mixed and you can lean back. Just relax. You said you want this on your left thigh, right?"

"Yes." She nods.

I grab the blacks and grays I'm going to need to do her tattoo, and then I set up her space. Getting the tattoo gun ready is my favorite part, and I take a deep breath and stretch out my hands before starting. She surprises me by not flinching when the gun touches her skin. She's less jumpy than I anticipated, and it's going to make my job a hell of a lot easier. Kate's quiet while I tattoo her, and I know better than to start up unwanted chatter.

I stay quiet as I think about how the hell I'm going to keep lying to my parents about this holiday drama. Would they pressure me to meet her? I doubt it. It's been years since I dated anyone. I try to recall if they had asked to meet my ex, but I think I was the one who had pushed for that interaction. At the time, I had wanted my parents to get to know the woman I thought I was going to marry. That moment in time seems so far away now. Here I am years later, and I can't believe that woman is the same one responsible for my Medusa tattoo. I don't know why I'm thinking about this. I wish she didn't pop into my head randomly like this. It's like I can't control it sometimes.

Kate takes a deep breath, pulling me back into the present, and I relax. I don't need to think about my ex right now. I just need to focus on this tattoo.

Finishing the outline, I give us both a quick break before jumping back in. It'll probably take me another hour before I complete this piece. The level of detail she wants is definitely a bit intricate. I keep going, trying to finish before I lose momentum. I zone out on the tattoo; sometimes tattooing becomes second nature to me, and I can do it without thinking much about it. It's something I love about my job. After a bit, I focus and realize I'm just about done. I put on the final touches and wipe off the blood and excess ink with a wet paper towel.

"You're all set," I say with a small smile.

"Oh my gosh, I love it!" She has tears brimming in her eyes as she looks at it.

"It's what you wanted?" I check.

"Yes, it's perfect. Can you take a picture of it for me?"

"Of course." I smile. I snap a few shots at a few different angles as she beams from ear to ear.

"Thank you so much." She jumps off the table, and I wrap her thigh to protect the tattoo. She hands me a twenty and quietly says, "This is all I have right now."

"Don't worry about it." I smile handing her back the money. I'm not in a spot where I technically need a job, so cutting people some slack when it comes to tattoos makes me feel better about it.

"I'll definitely be coming back." She smiles and heads out the front door.

"She looks happy," Addison muses.

"She does." I smile.

"A woman wants something simple drawn up for her but

Carter and Reagan don't have time. She was looking over your style and said she'd be happy with you."

"Sounds good, what's her name?"

"Sophie."

"Okay, Sophie you can come on back," I say a little louder to the blonde who's still looking through our tattoo books. They hold sheets of past tattoos that we've done as well as some artwork from tattoos we'd like to do.

"Hi!" she says a little too cheerily.

"So you're looking for me to draw you something?" I ask as I close the door behind her.

"Yes, I want a dancer on my hip. My stupid ex hated tattoos, but I just dumped his slimy ass and this is my way of reclaiming my body. Plus, I'm a dancer, so I thought I should commemorate that," she explains more than she needs to.

"Gotcha." This girl had so much to say that it took me a moment to realize how hot she is. I'm not one to flirt with customers, but damn. She has a dancer's thin physique, but she's also all muscle. Her long blonde hair is almost down to her ass, and her blue eyes pop. She's gorgeous. Not at all my type, if I'm being honest, but something about her makes me pause.

"Let me draw up a few sketches and see which one you like best." I smile. Then I turn on Spotify and play some indie music while I draw.

"You know Waterparks?!" She gasps.

"I do. I'm surprised you do," I say, looking up from my iPad.

"I'm a dancer, we did one of their songs at a performance last year," she explains. "It's kind of part of my job to know all sorts of music."

"Ah, do you work here in town?" I ask, knowing there's a dance studio right by the place we often got our coffee, Cinnamon Roll Saviors.

"I do. I actually co-own Moore Moves with my best friend, Delilah." She smiles proudly.

"That's cool." I look back at my iPad and hold it up for her to see. I drew four different dancers in different poses so she can pick one.

"Number three. That's definitely my vibe."

"Perfect. I'll draw it up more professionally and then get you started. Is this your first tattoo?"

"It is. That's okay, right?"

"Of course. I might use the numbing cream on your hip to help keep you comfortable."

"Okay." She nods.

"Why don't I do that now since it takes a little time to kick in?"

"Sure." She slides down her leggings and panties to the side, giving me a view of her hipbone. I put on a pair of gloves, rub the numbing cream gently over her hip, and tell her to wait like that so she doesn't smudge it on her clothes.

Chapter 4
Sophie

I look at the tattoo Lynn is drawing up, and I can't wait to have it tattooed on my body. It had started out as a big fuck you to my ex, but now this is just for me. It's not like anyone else is going to see it...unless I'm naked in front of them. Lynn will obviously see it too, because she's the one tattooing me. She's cute though. I wouldn't mind being naked in front of her. *Whoa, where did that come from?* It isn't lost on me that women are beautiful—like Lynn with her curves, tattoos, and her grumpy demeanor, but I'm not, like, *into* women. Sure, my best friend Delilah and I had kissed on more than one occasion when we were drunk, but we just have a close friendship.

"So this might hurt a little but if you need a break or anything just ask; there's no time limit here," Lynn explains.

"Okay." I nod. She puts the tattoo gun to my hip, and it hurts, but it's only a dull pinch. I thought it was going to hurt a ton more, so I'm grateful.

"What other bands do you like?" she asks, probably trying to keep my attention away from the tattoo.

"Familypet, the Front Bottoms, and AJR," I say proudly, although I assume she hasn't heard of them before.

"Ummm, I love the Front Bottoms," she says, her eyes widening.

"You do!?" I exclaim.

"I saw them in concert in Portland a few years back, they were so good."

"Me too! Oh my gosh! Were we at the same concert?" I laugh.

"Maybe." She smiles. It's nice. I can tell she's not someone who smiles often, but when she does, it lights up the room. It makes me want to make her smile all the time.

"Do you have a favorite song?" she asks.

"I love their newer stuff. It makes me wanna yell it while I drive in the car," I explain.

"Oh yeah, I can feel that. Something about it makes me wanna drive with the windows down and blast it for the world to hear."

"Exactly!"

"But also, I love the song 'Twin Size Mattress.'"

"Oh that's such a good one!" I gush.

"Here, I'll play some." She takes off her gloves and switches the music overhead, turning it up a bit louder. We're both singing along while she puts on a new pair of gloves and goes back to tattooing me. I'm having so much fun, I had forgotten I was even being tattooed.

I look at Lynn again, and I notice her lips are painted with a dark cherry lipstick, and her dark eye shadow only emphasizes her eyes. She has a bit more of a gothic vibe than I have, but I love that we have the same taste in music. That's something I never had with any of my exes. It's also way too easy to talk to her—almost like we've known each other for as long as I've known Delilah. Even she and I can't always talk this easily. Is this what it feels like to have a crush on someone of the same sex? I've never labeled myself, and I've always just dated whoever made my heart flutter. But right now, that's Lynn. All I want to do is ask her out and get to know her better.

"Okay, how's this looking so far?" she asks, and I twist my body to look at the tattoo.

"It looks fantastic! Can we make her skirt a light pink?"

"Of course." She nods and goes back to work on finishing up the tattoo. Then she's mixing colors and pouring them into these tiny cups and making a light pink for the skirt.

"So, do you work here every day?" I ask, knowing it's a lame attempt at 'you come here often' but I don't exactly know how to ask her out. I'm a bit out of my realm.

"I do. I work full time, and I kind of couldn't imagine doing anything else. I was one of the first people hired at the shop, and we all joke that I live here." She cracks a small smile.

"Oh, wow. I guess I'm the same way when it comes to the studio. Delilah usually has to kick me out when it's time for me to go home," I joke.

"Yeah, I'm usually here from noon to close. Reagan, the owner, lets us make our own hours."

"Do you ever have a day off to say, see a partner?" Wow, that came out super lame.

"I do have days off but I don't have a girlfriend if that's what you're asking." She glances up at me from tattooing and gives me a questioning look but doesn't ask what I'm thinking.

"I see," I mumble quietly. My confidence is suddenly nowhere to be found, and I don't know how to proceed. Flirting with men is so much easier; there's nothing to lose. But god, women are fucking intimidating.

"I'm almost done," she says, filling the silence.

"Perfect!" I say, smiling ear to ear. I'm losing time to make my move but I don't even know what I want to ask. *Hey, do you wanna fuck sometime?* I'm not some kind of fuck boy but I'm instantly attracted to her, and I do want to get a chance to kiss those cherry lips.

"Do you wanna do something sometime?" I ask way too fast, and my words get all jumbled together.

"What?" She looks at me with wide eyes.

"Do you want to hang out sometime outside of this tattoo shop?" I pause. "You just seem really cool, and you're hot, and I thought we got along pretty well...but also, don't feel inclined to say yes."

"I don't normally make a habit of hanging out with clients outside of work," she says, and my face falls. I can't help it, but it made sense. "But I'd really like it. You seem hella cool yourself, and you're gorgeous," she adds with a sly smile.

"Here." I pull her hand toward me and grab a pen out of my bag to write my phone number on her arm. It proves to be more difficult than I anticipate because she's covered in tattoos. I end up finding an empty spot, and I write my number and name where she can see it.

"Perfect." She nods. "Now, I just need to finish this shading."

"Of course." I grin and suddenly feel even better about this. She finishes up my tattoo, and I love the way it comes out. It's better than I could have even imagined.

Lynn takes a few photos of it, and I have her take a few with my phone, too. It's still red, but I can do some light editing and post it later tonight and make sure my shitty ex sees it before I block his ass.

"Thank you. It's honestly perfect." I smile at Lynn.

"I'm glad. You can pay at the front, and I'll be sure to text you when I'm done tonight," Lynn says.

"Sounds great."

She opens the door, and I head toward the reception area. I

leave a hearty tip for Lynn just because I love the way the tattoo came out. Walking out of the tattoo shop, I feel a little bit giddy at the idea of getting a text from Lynn later. I put my ringer on so I won't miss any notifications, and I drive toward the dance studio.

First things first, I need to see my best friend and show her my tattoo. And gush about the fact that I made a first move with a woman. This calls for a Taco Bell drive through night, but I know she has at least one more class to run through, so I'll hang out with her for a little bit there while I can.

When I make it inside Moore Moves, Delilah waves at me through the window and I drop my stuff off at the desk. There are a few parents waiting for their kids to come out of class, most of them on their phones. Our new hire, Fallon, is at the front desk helping someone sign up for a new class. She's a dancer as well as receptionist. We all kind of do a little bit of everything around here. We initially hired Fallon to be here during Delilah's maternity leave. We brought her on about six months ago after dozens of applications, and she was definitely the best fit for us. Now that Delilah is back from maternity leave, we've made a permanent place for her at Moore Moves.

"Hey, I just filled up the 4-5 year old class so we have to make a note on the website," Fallon says coming over to me.

"Sounds good, make me a note on my desk and I'll do it in the morning. I'm not technically here."

"I didn't think so." She laughs. "Waiting for Delilah?"

"Yup!" I nod.

"She should be done in fifteen minutes, then I have my adult jazz class," she explains happily.

"Perfect, and things went well all last night being on your own?" I ask. It was her first time being on her own. Delilah and I thought she could handle it but we still like to check in.

"It went great! I left out a sign-up sheet at the front desk in case anybody needed anything, and a few parents signed up for new classes that way. I called them back after my class and helped them with the process. Plus my class was great." She explains as she ties up her dark black hair in a tight pony.

"Great." I smile and head back to my office that I share with Delilah. I can see her class on the cameras we had installed, and she's doing cool downs now.

Fifteen minutes later, Delilah is in the office, looking for her ice water. I hand her the oversized cup and she smiles, sucking down all the water.

"Please tell me you're here because you want some Taco Bell," she says with a cheesy smile.

"I am! But I also wanted to show you this." I pull my leggings down on the side so she can see my new tattoo. It's taped up but you can still see it through the tattoo tape.

"Wow! It's about damn time! You'll have to tell me all about it over tacos. Your car or mine?" she asks, gushing over it. I can tell she's hungry, and she'll listen better when there's food in front of her.

We pile into my car and twenty minutes later we're parked outside the Taco Bell closest to town. Delilah is munching on a taco, and I pop a chip in my mouth. Nothing beats greasy Taco Bell with my best friend.

"So, tell me, what's up?" Taco Bell is also code for we *need to talk*. And what better way to break big news than over delicious food?

"So I broke up with Kyle," I start.

"It's about damn time. Oh my gosh! That's why you finally got a tattoo, right? Because you broke up with him?" She looks more excited than I expected but it's also not super surprising. She was never his biggest fan, but I hadn't realized how much she didn't like him.

"I mean part of it, yes," I admit.

"Okay, breakup tattoos are what the vibe is. I've been there." She points to the rose on her forearm. She's covered in tattoos. Not so much as some of the women I've seen, but she does have a lot.

"But there's something else I need to tell you." I pause for dramatic effect. "I have a date with the hot tattoo artist."

"That's amazing! I'm glad you're getting back out there but that was Taco Bell worthy news?" She looks at me confused.

"It's with a *female* tattoo artist."

Her eyes become as wide as saucers. "Oh my gosh! This is so amazing! Definitely Taco Bell worthy." She gushes.

"And I'm the one who asked *her* out."

"Whoa! That's so amazing, though! Girls are so different but fun in the best of ways. If I wasn't with Ryan, I'd date women again," she admits with a shrug. I've known about Delilah being bisexual for a long time, so it's nothing new to me.

"Pretty sure you're stuck with Ryan, at least for now," I tease, thinking about my nieces.

"Happily stuck." She smiles. "So! Tell me all about the girl!"

I'm glad Delilah isn't making this feel like a huge *coming out* thing. The last thing I need to do is label myself.

Chapter 5

Lynn

I look at the number on my arm and think about what to do. I don't make a habit out of flirting with my clients, and I don't think it was obvious how cute I thought she was. But maybe I was being too forward without realizing it? I pull out my phone and save the number to a new contact: *Sophie*. Then I click on the texting button and try to type up a text. I mean, what am I supposed to say? I never do this kind of thing, that's why I'm eternally single.

"Whatcha doing? You look stressed," my boss and friend, Reagan, says as she slides into the tattoo chair across from me.

"A girl gave me her number today, and I told her I'd text her but I don't know what to say," I admit.

"Oh yeah! This is so exciting. You never go out with anyone," Reagan says. It's so ironic coming from her because before her now husband came back into town, she was as single as I was.

"I mean, I don't *not* go out with people." I shrug. "I don't always have the best experiences when it comes to dating, so it takes a lot for me to want to go out with someone.

"Well, think of it this way...you're only texting. It's not like it means you have to go out with her or something," Reagan points out.

"That's true." I hadn't realized that.

"Just give her one of those *hey it's Lynn* texts and see what she says. If she gave you her number she's probably going to take the lead anyway."

"Okay." I let out a sigh and type it quickly, pressing send before I can overthink it.

Lynn: Hey it's Lynn.
Sophie: Hiiii! How'd the rest of your day go?

"Oh shit. She texted back already." My eyes widen.

"That's a good thing! What did she say?" I tilt the phone toward her so she can look at the text.

"See, she'll definitely lead the conversation if you let her." Reagan nods.

"It's just been so long since I've *talked* to someone like this," I admit.

"But it's a good thing, even if it doesn't go anywhere, you've got experience from it." Reagan smiles.

"That's true."

"Don't overthink it! I have to head out but I want to hear all about it tomorrow." She waves and heads out the front door of the shop.

I'm used to nights here by myself, and it's actually something I prefer. I can close up, taking my sweet time, and set up for the morning. This is perfect for me because it means I get to sleep in just a little bit longer. I'm more of a night owl anyway, and I love to catch those late night clients looking for a tattoo.

Only for the Holidays

It's great that Reagan let me stay open as late as I want, everyone else has family or kids to get home to, but I love staying late. I've noticed the new girl, Carter, stays late sometimes, too, but it's often just until her girlfriend gets out of work.

"Just text her back," I mumble to myself.

LYNN: It was good! Lots of clients so my hand is killing me. Time for the massager when I get home. Hby?

Sophie: Ooo a massager? 😏 sounds like my kind of night.

Is this girl flirting with me? I hadn't meant one of *those* massagers, not that I don't have a nice collection of vibrators at home. I'm single and some of those things can make me come harder than another person ever could.

SOPHIE: Don't worry I'm just joking. I was out with my bestie, and we got Taco Bell. Now I'm headed home for the night.

Lynn: Taco Bell sounds bomb right now. Might have to make a drive out just for a chalupa.

Sophie: Don't tempt me with a good time, I could never say no to Taco Bell.

Lynn: Even if you already had it today?

Sophie: Hey, don't judge my love of tacos.

Lynn: No judgement here, don't worry.

I PUT my phone down so I can start cleaning up the shop. Taking my time, I clean up my room first and then give the front room a little bit of tidying. It isn't too bad, but I like it to look nice when everyone comes in the morning. I'm off tomorrow so I don't need to set up for the morning but I prepare everything else.

My phone buzzes in my pocket again, and I reach for it, seeing two texts from Sophie.

Sophie: Good, if you were judging it would be hard to ask you out.
Sophie: Shit, too forward?

Lynn: Is that your way of asking me out?
Sophie: It might be, I'm sort of new to this. I don't normally ask women out.
Lynn: I imagine they ask you out quite often though.
Sophie: You'd be surprised. I've been on a strictly dickly diet for a while but I think I want to change that...
Lynn: So are you asking me on a date or to come over?
Sophie: Depends on what your answer would be.

I pause. I don't normally hang out with experimenting women. I have no problem with bisexual women, but I don't want to be anyone's so called *experiment*. But then again, Sophie is freaking beautiful. Even if she turns out to just be a one-night stand, I think we'd both be in for a treat.

Lynn: I think you should come over.
Sophie: Now?

Only for the Holidays

Lynn: Tomorrow?
Sophie: It's a not date

♡♡♡

I HAVE the day off which is terrible for my nerves. I sleep in until noon but then I'm sipping my coffee and lounging on the couch, thinking about Sophie. And the fact that I was bold enough to invite her over tonight? I never do that kind of thing. Not that I'm opposed to one-night stands, but I don't know. I haven't had a lot of them. Last night we both stayed up until three a.m. just texting and getting to know each other better. I learned she has an older brother, two nieces, and a pretty strict family—just like mine. She's been a dancer all her life, and she makes most of her money on TikTok, although she wouldn't share the link of her account with me. But I know I'll be able to get it out of her when she's ready. I mean, I'm basically a stranger, but to was nice that I knew her a little better since she was coming over.

I look around my place and realize I'll have to do some major cleaning before Sophie comes over. Not that I intend to spend much time in the living room, I mean, isn't she just coming over for a hookup? Still, I want the place to look like I didn't forget to clean all week long. It's hard when I work full-time. Even simple things like the dishes sometimes get overlooked.

I sip my coffee and sigh, knowing after I finish this cup, I'll make a go of it and tidy everything up before Sophie comes. *Arrives.* Whatever.

Furball jumps up on the couch, and I have a realization that hits me like a ton of bricks. What if Sophie is allergic to cats? I wouldn't even know what to do if that was the case. I quickly send her a text to ask how she feels about cats.

SOPHIE: Love 'em!
   Lynn: Not allergic, then?
   Sophie: Not at all 😊

THANK GOODNESS. What would I have done if she was allergic to Furball? One of my exes was and always insisted Furball sleep in another room at night. But I got lonely, and thinking back, I wish it was my ex who had slept in the other room. I pet Furball with my free hand and sip my coffee with the other.

"I'm having company tonight, Furball. But you have to be nice, because we're going to be doing some grown up things."

Furball looks at me, confused, and I smile. Sometimes I wish I could read her mind.

"Okay, I have to clean this place up," I tell myself and Furball.

I place my cup in the sink and decide to start with the dishes. I roll up my sleeves and dig into the week-old dishes that have been accumulating. Once I'm done with those, I tackle the laundry and the vacuuming. I tidy around the house, moving things and then putting them back. I'm clearly overthinking this, but whatever. I'm just nervous about Sophie coming over for the first time. By the time I'm done cleaning, it's almost time for Sophie to arrive so I hop in the shower and shave my entire body. It isn't exactly easy for someone plus sized. I love my body, but I wish my shower was a little bigger or I could be a little bit more flexible. Why is it only during sex that my body is able to bend in such ways that I can't during the day?

Only for the Holidays

I eat a quick dinner after my shower and then brush my teeth again, just in case. I'm trying not to read too much into what might happen tonight, but from the way Sophie was texting, it seems very likely we'll be having sex. It's equally exciting and nerve-racking Having sex with someone new is always a little awkward at first. It isn't like being in a relationship or friends with benefits where the person knows exactly how to please you. Come to think of it, I'm having second thoughts about this one-night stand. But fuck it, how bad could it possibly be to hook up with such a beautiful woman? Before I can answer my rhetorical question, the doorbell rings and I let out a deep breath.

Looking down at the outfit I've chosen, I hope it's casual enough. It's my lucky black tee and a pair of distressed ripped black jeans. I'm wearing a matching panty and bra set just in case we do have sex. I want to be prepared but not too prepared —like wearing lingerie. I fix my thong from sticking in my butt, in the bad way, and make my way to the front door. Furball goes to hide, as she does every time the front door opens.

I open the door, and on my front porch is a beautiful blonde holding a bottle of wine. She has a wide smile on her face. She's often smiling, but this time her smile is for me. It almost feels *special* in a way. She holds out the bottle of wine to me and begins rambling.

"I was going to bring wine and then I thought maybe you don't drink, but I drink, and so I brought flowers but that felt too romantic so I thought I'd go with a snack but I didn't know if you had any allergies so I went back to the wine and figured if you don't drink then we don't have to drink." She lets out a deep sigh and smiles again. Her pink lips over white, straight teeth make me wonder if she ever had braces or she was genetically blessed.

"I drink wine," I say awkwardly.

"Can I come in?" She peers in the doorway, and I realize I've been staring at her so long that I forgot to invite her inside.

"Oh my gosh! Of course. Please, come in." She steps inside and looks around. "Furball— my cat, is around here somewhere," I tell her.

"Is she afraid of people?"

"Just new people."

"Me too," Sophie says, and we both laugh. Standing in the doorway, I wonder if she feels as nervous as I do right now.

Chapter 6

Sophie

The minute Lynn invites me inside, my nerves skyrocket to the max. I'm about to have a one-night stand with a woman I barely know. Sure, Lynn seems cool, and I spent the night getting to know her, but I don't really *know* her. I mean she could be a serial killer for all I know. But Delilah convinced me to swallow my fears and go anyway—after sharing my location with her. And I'm glad I'm here, Lynn is every bit as hot as I remembered, and I'm totally still down. I'm just nervous.

I don't remember being this nervous before I lost my virginity. Sure, I was also fifteen in the back of my mom's minivan and just trying to make sure we didn't get caught. But still, this is like losing it all over again.

"We can open the bottle of wine and just watch a movie if you want? I have Netflix up if you wanna pick something." Lynn smiles softly. It's not as big as mine but more of a subtle happy. I guess she isn't nearly as nervous as I am.

Fuck, am I sweating? I can't control my nerves. I nod and follow her to the living room area while she stops in the kitchen to pour us some wine. I find the remote on the coffee table and look around the room.

There's a pale blue couch that forms an L-shape around half the room facing a large flat screen TV. She has two bookcases on the far wall near the outside doors, and they're full of photos and mementos. I want to take a closer look but I don't know how much time I have before she gets back. I can't help but compare her apartment to some of the men's apartments I've been in lately. There's a cozy feel about her place. There's a black Halloween blanket hanging on the couch and a cat scratching post for Furball—which is a very interesting name. I'll have to ask her why she chose that.

"Here you are." She hands me a glass of wine in one of those glasses without a stem, and I realize in my curiosity I forgot to pick anything out.

"Sorry, I didn't see anything good. I'm the worst at deciding what to watch," I lie.

"No worries, we can just put on something for background and talk?"

"Sure." I feel a little more comfortable as she sits next to me. Something about her presence is calming.

"*Friends?*" she asks.

"I love *Friends.*"

"Oh, me too! Who's your favorite?" Lynn asks, taking a sip of her wine.

"I love them all, but my friends always said I'm similar to Rachel so I think I'm partial to her." I laugh.

"I love Joey but Rachel is definitely hotter." Lynn winks and I almost choke on my wine. I had expected flirting, but up until now, I'd been the one making most of the moves.

"I've always had a crush on Monica; I think I'm partial to the brunettes." I wink back.

"Good to know." Lynn moves a little closer and looks at me. "Is this okay?"

"More than." I nod. I don't know if she's just moving closer or getting ready to make a move, but either way, I'm ready. I set down my wine glass on the table in front of me just in case.

"If you ever want me to stop, just say the word. We can play Scrabble or something," Lynn says.

"I appreciate that. But I think there's something else I'd rather we play."

Lynn looks at me with hooded eyes. She's exactly where I want her, and suddenly, all the nerves are gone. It's like something is awakening inside me. I lean into her just as she leans closer to me. Lynn's arm wraps around my shoulders and her other hand tangles in my hair. I close my eyes as our lips press together. We share a few small, chaste kisses to get our lips acquainted before she casually slips a tongue into my mouth. It swirls with mine, in a way that can only be described as Frenching. Her hand grips my hair gently, and I lean in closer, pulling her T-shirt toward me. Our bodies press against each other as a ferocity builds between us.

"Wow," Lynn says, pulling back breathlessly.

My sentiments exactly. What the hell had I been doing kissing men all that time? Sure it was good, but kissing Lynn is entirely different.

I lean in to kiss her again but this time we both bump heads.

"Ow." We both groan, holding our foreheads. We clunked pretty damn hard.

"I'm so sorry!" Lynn exclaims. "Do you need ice?"

"Nah, I think I'll be okay," I reassure her.

"Can we try that again?" she asks, and I nod. This time both of us keep our eyes open until we're closer to each other.

Our lips graze and our tongues dance together, twirling

into one. I feel all the nerves from before leaving my body, and all that's left in their place is an ease I can't describe.

We kiss for what feels like forever, both of us smiling when we come up for air every so often. It was like we can't get enough of each other's lips. It is addicting, kissing a *woman*, kissing *Lynn*.

"Do you want to head to my room?" Lynn asks after a while.

"Can I use your bathroom first?" I smile.

"Of course. Second door on the left." She points down the small hallway, and I excuse myself.

I pee, because the wine I drank seemed to go right through me. Then I look at my makeup in the mirror and make sure nothing is out of place. I glance at my phone, checking the texts from Delilah I missed.

DELILAH: You got this!

Delilah: Remember, eating pussy is just like sucking dick except it's totally different, but never use teeth!

Delilah: If you're nervous just follow her lead.

Delilah: Are you not answering because you're having sex?!

I SHOOT Delilah a quick text that no sex has been had but it might be about to happen, and then click off my phone. I don't want Lynn thinking I'm pooping in here.

I find Lynn's bedroom just down the hall, and she's checking her phone, lying in bed. She looks casual, not like she's expecting to have sex right now. It's almost like she's not anticipating anything, which makes it easier on me. I know I can stop this whenever I want, but with Lynn I was more and more curious about her and her body.

"Whatcha doing?" I ask, casually lying in the bed next to her. Fuck, it's comfortable.

"I was looking at some tattoo ideas and thinking about what I want to draw later." She tilts the phone toward me and shows me a beautiful looking floral piece.

"Did you do that?" I ask, impressed.

"Yup, a client of mine just posted it," she says proudly. She's incredibly talented. It's something I already knew but this only emphasizes it.

"You're very talented." I smile.

"I've heard you're pretty talented at dancing, too, but I haven't been shown any proof," she teases.

"Is that your way of asking for my TikTok?" I laugh. It isn't that I don't want to give it to her, but I don't want her to only see me as a dancer the way some people do. I want her to see all parts of me first.

"Maybe." She drags out the ending of the word and puts her phone down. Turning her body on its side, she faces me and brings one hand to my waist. She pulls me in closer, and I feel my breath hitch as our bodies press against each other. We're still fully clothed but the anticipation is driving me crazy.

Lynn kisses me first this time, our lips transcending each other's. I close my eyes and relax under her touch. She hums against my lips lightly, eliciting a small moan from me. Biting on my bottom lip, she drags it out and stares me in the eye for just a fleeting moment before letting go. And suddenly my core is on fire, and my panties are soaked. Never have I ever been so turned on so easily from another person.

"Let me know if you want to stop, I know you said you haven't had much experience with women, right?"

"Try no experience." I let out an awkward laugh.

"Okay, well I'll just follow your lead then." She smiles and kisses my cheek. She moves to my lips again and we're back to kissing. But this time I want more. She's awakened something in me.

I reach for the hem of her T-shirt and tug at it gently. I don't know what I want exactly, but just touching her doesn't seem like enough. I graze my hands over her covered breasts and squeeze gently. I hate when men honk and squeeze my boobs like they are trying to milk a cow. She moans quietly against my mouth, and I take that as an opportunity to reach for the other one. Her breasts spill out of my hands, and I feel the heat pooling in between my thighs.

She reaches for my neck and runs her fingertips down it, causing a chill down my spine. Lynn kisses me harder, and I tug at the bottom of her shirt again. This time, knowing what I want. I tug it halfway off her body before she sits up, and with our lips still attached, she throws it across the room. I pull away from her to sit up, and I look at the black lace bra she's wearing. Her tits are pale and overflowing from the cups, almost enough where I can see her nipples. Oh yeah, I'm fucking wet. I'm definitely into women.

"Like what you see?" Lynn doesn't hide her body, but instead embraces every curve and every inch. I take in all of her, her rolls and her body. She's absolutely beautiful.

"I do." I smirk and pull her in by the head for a longer kiss.

Our lips are otherwise occupied and my hands are all over her breasts. God, who knew it could be so much fun playing with boobs? She reaches for my shirt, and I let her pull it off me. I don't shy away from her either, I mean I'm confident in my body. But it's because I'm comfortable with Lynn. There's an ease about this, and I know I don't need to be nervous anymore. I love kissing her and touching her is something I clearly can't get enough of.

"You are beautiful," Lynn murmurs before kissing my neck.

I moan lightly as she does because fuck does that feel heavenly. Her lips press against the warm skin of my neck.

"Oh," I whisper when Lynn's cool hands find my breasts. They're nothing compared to hers; I barely fill out an A cup, but she seems to like them. She kneads them softly and dips her fingers just below the lace of my bralette to play with my nipple.

"Mmm," I mutter. She tugs gently, pulling it to harden under her touch before dipping her head lower and taking one in her mouth. I'm trying to focus on what she's doing so I can copy it but it feels too fucking good. I throw my head back in pleasure, and I can feel her smile against me.

"Oh, fuck," I whisper when she takes the second one in between her fingers before switching her tongue to tease that one too.

"I can't wait to taste you," Lynn mutters, and I swear if my panties weren't already soaked, they would be now.

Chapter 7

Lynn

I think this is the slowest I've ever taken to be intimate with another human. Not that I'm usually one to skip the foreplay but fuck I don't think I've ever had *this* much foreplay. Not that it's bothering me either; I don't mind going slow. I mean sure, I'm wet as hell and dying for a release, but I know it'll come with time. Either with Sophie, or if she isn't up for it, then later on with my vibrator.

"Can you take this off?" Sophie asks after struggling to take off my bra.

"Of course, it's harder when it's not on you."

"It really is!" she exclaims with a laugh. God I love the way she's so happy and positive. It's addicting.

I unclasp my bra, and my breasts fall to my stomach. They aren't perky like hers but the way she's looking at them tells me she doesn't mind. Her mouth goes to them like magnets. She takes a nipple in her mouth, similar to the way I did, but she flicks her tongue and I moan. She's inexperienced with women? That didn't seem like a rookie trick. I'm gasping as she's tugging

Only for the Holidays

with my other nipple and playing with the metal bar between her fingers.

"I love your piercings," she gushes. Then instantly they're back in her mouth, her tongue sliding over the metal bar as I cry out in pleasure. Fuck, her tongue feels good.

"You seem more experienced than you've let on."

"I mean, I've had experience with my tongue. I'm just following your sounds." She blushes. It's an adorable pink creeping over her cheeks.

"Well, it's definitely working for me." I laugh and bite my bottom lip with a moan. She's looking me in the eye with her pretty blues while tugging on my nipples with both hands. It's inherently sexy, and I want to flip her on the bed and eat her pussy until she's begging me to stop. But I'm following her lead, so I reach for her bra and unclasp it with one hand.

"Show off," she murmurs, and we both laugh.

"Practice," I say with a small shrug. Her breasts had already been peeking out of the lace, and sure there isn't much of them, but that is okay with me. I just like providing the pleasure in any way I can.

"I think I want you to touch me," she whispers quietly.

"You think?" I clarify, that wasn't exactly a yes.

"No, I definitely want you to touch me. I want you to have your way with me. I trust you."

"Just say the word, and we'll stop," I remind her.

"Very unlikely." She laughs.

I push her back into the pillows, and her blonde hair cascades down her shoulders. She looks like a dream, something I want to take a moment to capture, just in case this never happens again. Even though I want it to happen again. We haven't even had sex yet but damn do I want to devour her completely. I tug down on her leggings and look at her lace-covered pussy. She's desperately soaked, and I almost growl at how sexy that is. I've barely touched her and she *wants* me.

I climb over to kiss her again, this time slow and sensual. Taking her tongue between my teeth gently, just enough to suck on it, and she moans in my mouth. I place wet, open mouthed kisses down her neck, her chest, her flat stomach, all the way to her core. I can smell her arousal growing in anticipation of what I'm about to do. Fuck, my mouth waters just at the thought of tasting her.

"Is this okay?" I ask again.

"Mmm, more than okay. Yes." She nods reverently and I giggle. It's cute how much she wants this, and I love that she's giving me her first time with a woman. It's not something I'm overlooking. I want this to be as good for her as it will be for me.

I press a kiss to her pussy through her lace panties, and she moans, her hips bucking to my face instantly. Fuck. She's responsive as hell. She wants this more than I realized. I kiss her a few more times, pushing down her hips each time until I decide to stop teasing us both. I clench my thighs together to help the ache between them. Then I pull down her panties, her hips rising instantly to help them down her legs.

"Fuck," I mutter under my breath. She's fucking beautiful. This might be the prettiest pussy I've ever seen.

"What?" She looks at me nervously.

"You have a beautiful pussy," I say aloud. She turns a bright red and covers her face with her hands.

Instead of saying anything else, I dive in and take a long, languid lick of her pussy. She shivers at the touch of my tongue, and I hold onto her hips to steady her. Licking from clit to hole, I swirl my tongue around in her juices. She tastes even sweeter than I anticipated. I lap up all of her while sucking lightly on her clit, and she squirms under me.

Only for the Holidays

"Oh, fuck," she mutters. Her breath is heavy and unsteady. Is she that close already? I've barely done anything.

I run two fingers up and down her soaked pussy. She pushes my head down closer to her core, and I lick furiously with her thighs wrapping around my head. I push two fingers inside her, and I can feel her clenching down around my fingers. She's close and this is going to be a good one if the way she's holding on to the sheets is any indication. I flick my tongue over her sensitive bud and curl my fingers at the same time, creating a waterfall.

"Oh, fuck!" she screams out. "Oh, Lynn!" She squirts all over my face, pushing my hand away. Sophie drenches my sheets, and I don't even care. There's nothing I love more than making a woman orgasm like that.

I wipe my face off casually with the top sheet and climb up to lie next to Sophie while she comes down from her orgasm. Her breathing is heavy, and her eyes are still clamped shut while she bites down on her bottom lip. God she's never looked better.

"You okay?" I ask with a smirk. I know how she's feeling, but it's still adorable to watch her come undone like that.

"I'm fucking fantastic." She breathes out. "I knew I could squirt, I've made myself do it, but fuck...no one else has ever been able to."

"I'll take that as a compliment." I smile. I'm still aching for a release, but I want to see how Sophie does. This was her first time with a woman, and I want to check in. I mean, that was a big change for her, but she seems to be doing fine.

"What about you? Do you want a turn?" Sophie looks nervous.

"If you want to, I won't say no. But don't do anything you aren't ready for."

41

"Is it okay if I try it next time? I just think tonight was a lot already for me."

"Of course." I smile. I had hoped there would be a next time too, but I didn't want to be the first one to say it out loud.

"So, now what do you usually do?"

"Well, I'm going to change the sheets. But we can shower if you want, or we can just cuddle. It's kind of late so you're welcome to stay over. It's up to you," I suggest. Something about this woman is making me want to hold her in my arms. Even just for a little. I usually cuddle after sex, but I don't typically initiate it.

"A shower sounds like a lot of work right now, can we just cuddle?" she asks, looking at me. Her blue eyes seem to get bigger when she wants something.

"Sure, I'll grab some fresh sheets." I head down the hall to the bathroom closet and grab a fresh set of sheets.

"I'm sorry I ruined your sheets," she mutters with a pink over her cheeks again.

"Please, they're not ruined they just need a good washing, and I would happily do that again to you." I wave her worries off.

Sophie helps me make the bed and then surprises me by picking up my T-shirt. I think she's going to hand it to me but instead she slides it on and wears it as a night shirt. We're not exactly the same size so it falls to her upper thigh and reminds me she's not wearing any panties. Is this how men feel when women wear their clothes? Because something about it being my favorite is making me want to eat her out again. But instead, I grab myself a clean shirt, change my panties, and climb into bed next to her.

"Come here," I tell her and hold out my arm. She snuggles in my chest, and I can smell the scent of her shampoo, something and avocados. It's nice, subtle.

"That was a lot of fun," she says quietly.

"I'm glad you had fun. Maybe next time we can try some other things," I say mischievously.

"Like what?" Her eyes gleam up at me in curiosity.

"I mean like toys. I have a strap on and vibrators. Whatever you want to try."

"Ooo, yes please. The most I've ever done with someone else was when my ex tied me up for the thirty seconds before he came. So disappointing."

"Well, if we continue doing this we can explore together. Figure out what you like and don't like. Like friends with benefits."

"I would love that. Oh my gosh, that sounds like so much fun." She smiles hugely, and I can't help but smile, too, at the thought of all the things I want to do to her. I squirm a bit, pressing my thighs together again. I'm in deep need of a release but I know I'll have to wait until tomorrow to get one.

Sophie snuggles in my chest, and I can hear her breathing change. She's quiet and then she's sleeping. I don't blame her. She had one intense orgasm and probably a long ass day. I rub her hair with my hand, and she begins to snore lightly. It's something I'll have to tease her about when she gets up. I close my eyes and start to doze when I hear a light moan. Is she... having a sex dream? No. Maybe I just thought I heard something. But then there it is again. Sophie moans and her body moves against mine, and I'm in serious torture for how horny I am in this moment.

So, I slide my body away from Sophie's, grab my vibrator from my nightstand, and sneak to the bathroom down the hall. There's a bathroom in my room but I don't want her to wake up and hear me. I pull down my panties, and I'm soaked again. My pussy is dripping so I turn the vibrator on to the highest setting, let it suck on my clit, and wait for the orgasm to hit. I think about how sexy Sophie is, how beautiful her body is, and how she sounds when she's coming. It only takes minutes before I'm clamping a hand over my mouth to keep from screaming out.

    I sneak back into bed after washing my hands and hiding my toy. Then I slide Sophie's body next to mine again, and it's like I never left. Sophie's snores put me to sleep as I think about how nice it is to have someone in my bed again.

Chapter 8

Sophie

"Can you put on a sweater, dear? We don't all need to see your midriff," my mother says with a sigh as she looks over my clothing choice. In my defense, I had forgotten I was coming over after work or I would've put on something else entirely. And it isn't like my *entire* stomach is hanging out; it's just a little sliver.

"Sure." I sigh and grab one from the hall closet. I know better than to argue with my mother on family dinner night. She would have a cow if anything didn't go according to her perfect plan. It's kind of irritating but it's something my brother and I accept.

She's kind of old fashioned in her values and from the way she was raised. It's a miracle I turned out the way I did. But then again, I've always been the black sheep in my family.

"Auntie Sophie!" My niece, Jesse, runs to my legs while her sister, Jemma, stands back with her stuffed rabbit. They couldn't be more opposite if they tried. I scoop them both up for a big hug and kiss them both before putting them down on the ground.

"It's so good to see you girls." I smile. They're the real reason I make it to family dinner every weekend.

"Daddy's in the car, he said he had to get something," Jesse explains with a shrug before running off.

"Hey! I'm here! Sorry, I had to grab the girls backpacks. Thanks again for watching them tonight." My brother, Montgomery, smiles. He places the backpacks by the door and greets me with a hug.

"Hi, big bro." I smile.

"Hi, Sissy. How's it going?" he asks, looking around the room. Mom's in the kitchen preparing dinner, and Dad is in the living room watching his football.

"Mom's being Mom, I'm here for my favorite nieces."

"They're your only nieces."

"Uh, Delilah's babies would beg to differ," I point out. She's basically my sister so I would be nothing other than Auntie Sophie to those babies.

"Did Delilah ever get remarried yet?" my mother asks, holding a bowl and mixing the contents slowly.

"Nope, I think they're waiting." I know how my mother feels about this. She's made it all too clear that my best friend shouldn't be having babies out of wedlock. It's not like she was some teenage mother, although nothing wrong with that either. She just wants to wait until she and Ryan know each other better. They've both been married before and don't want to be divorced a second time before they're thirty-five. But I can't tell my mother that.

"I don't know what they're waiting for, they're not getting any younger." She shakes her head in disapproval.

"It's better than they get married and divorced again," I point out. This time she stays silent, and I know it's because my brother is here. His wife divorced him a few months ago after leaving out of the blue almost two years ago. He was an absolute mess after that, so I know my mother knows better than to say anything about it.

"When are you bringing Kyle over again? He was such a sweetheart," my mother says, clearly changing the subject. This is when I suck in and brace myself for impact.

"Actually, I've been meaning to tell you. Kyle and I broke up."

"What? Why? You two were so great together."

"I'm going to check on the girls." Monty excuses himself, and I glare at him from behind. I needed backup right now, not a coward.

"We weren't so great together." I can't tell my mother I broke up with the "perfect guy" because he couldn't make me orgasm. I think she might have a heart attack.

"You always do this, a guy seems great, and you end it—like with Luke or Jeremy. They were great guys, and then *poof*. You're not getting any younger, you know." She points the spoon full of mashed potatoes at me.

"They weren't great guys for me. I want someone who makes me happy, Mom, and they just didn't. Even if they were 'great' guys,'" I point out.

"Ugh." She sighs and heads back into the kitchen just in time for my brother to return.

"I could've used some help with Mom." I sigh.

"I know, I'm sorry. I just have some news of my own today, and I have to keep her on my good side for once." He frowns.

"What news?" I raise an eyebrow.

"I've hired a nanny. And I know how Mom feels about help outside the family, but I've been drowning between work and the girls and everything. I need the extra help," he says with an exasperated sigh.

"Monty, if you're struggling you can always ask me. I'm

happy to take time off work to watch the girls." I reach for his arm and he smiles.

"Thank you, but it's more than that, and I think this is what I want to do. She starts next Monday so I need to tell Mom now before the girls do."

"I understand, I'll have your back."

"Dinner's served!" my mother calls, and we all make our way to the dining room.

The girls sit between Monty and I while our parents take each head of the table. It's a full course meal, and I expect nothing less from my mom. She's a bit of an overachiever when it comes to *homemaking*, as she calls it. She wants to pass the trait down to me but I have no interest in it. There's no way I would ever be cooking meals for some man like it's 1952 and putting his napkin on his lap like he doesn't have two hands to do it himself. My husband—or wife or partner—and I will split the responsibilities.

Not that my parents know that. Sure, it's new but it definitely isn't something I'm going to tell my parents about either. They are far too traditional to understand that I might not be marrying a man and giving them grandkids in a traditional way. I shake my head, trying to think of anything else; I don't want to start a world war tonight. I just want to get through the night with as little attention on me as possible.

"So, Mom, Dad," Monty starts.

"Girls, please no elbows on the table," my mom says. "Yes, Montgomery?"

"I have some news."

"Oh?" my dad mumbles while chewing away at the chicken my mom baked.

"I've decided to hire a nanny to help out with the girls."

Clang!

My mother drops her fork from her mouth, and it hits the

plate. Monty looks at me, but I'm just as surprised by my mother's reaction. If there's one thing you could expect from Mom, it's short responses and not a major reaction. She's clearly been thrown off guard, which is hard to do. She picks up her fork and grinds her teeth into a smile, looking at the girls before she replies.

"I wish you would've come to me had you needed more help."

"I know, but I think this is better for everyone."

"Hiring a stranger is somehow better? What they need is a mother."

"Mom," I snap. That was a low blow.

The girls are completely oblivious, munching away on their food while my mother continues.

"What? I'm just being real. They don't need a stranger coming in and telling them how it is. They need to be surrounded by *family*."

"Well, I think what Monty is doing is great. He's doing what's best in his eyes for them, and we should just all respect it."

"Respect? You want to talk about respect?" Her voice sharpens. At least the focus is on me instead of my brother.

"Margaret," my dad says in a warning tone, and everyone goes silent. It's rare my dad has anything to say, and on the occasions he does, it's not usually pleasant. It's usually a chance to yell at someone. So for it to be directed at Mom, we are all shocked into silence.

"Fine. More peas?" My mother does a deep sigh and changes the subject once again. My dad looks at me and winks when no one else is looking. At least he's still on my side.

After dinner we all help my mother clean up. And by us "cleaning up" I mean we put the dishes in the sink and then she kicks us out of the kitchen until dessert is ready. We all gather in the living room to watch football with my dad and the girls color in the corner on their little table. Monty and I have a chance to talk since my dad is so focused on the game.

"I thought you were a goner in there," I whisper.

"Well thanks for your help, it's not lost on me. I'm sorry Mom is so hard on you." He frowns. I just shrug, I'm used to it. For whatever reason, I'm not my mother's favorite. Even when she's mad at Monty, I know she'll be over it in no time.

"Dessert time!" my mother calls. The girls go running, for which my mother berates them for, and then they take their seats.

My mom makes the best homemade apple pie in the world. Another reason I come for Sunday night dinners. I dig in and listen to my family make small talk about things that won't upset the other. It's kind of sad that we all have to walk on eggshells and monitor what we say instead of saying what we want to. But that's my family.

I start to think about Lynn and if her family is the same way. We haven't talked too much about families because I don't want to bring up mine. It's nice hanging out with Lynn, and I don't want to pop that bubble just yet. Sure, we're just friends with benefits, but I don't know, isn't it possible that some day we could be more? I don't know where that thought came from. Maybe because of how beautiful Lynn is, or how good she is at making me orgasm. I'm falling for her more than I had originally planned.

"Sophie? Are you bringing anyone to Thanksgiving next week?" my mother asks.

"Oh, umm..." I think about Lynn and bringing her. But I could never ask that of her, even though I'd love to watch my mother's eyes pop out of her head. Seeing me with a woman, a tattooed woman, nonetheless, would be enough to send her into cardiac arrest.

"No, I don't think so." I sigh. I can't put Lynn through that, and besides we're just friends with benefits. It's not like we're dating or anything.

"That's too bad. Maybe I'll have to invite Tommy from next door, he's always asking about you," she says as if that's not creepy. He's almost ten years older than me and used to spy on me when I was a teenager.

"No, thank you." I shake my head. "I can find my own person to bring for Thanksgiving," I lie.

"Oh goodie! Just let me know who it is so I can make up a place card with their name on it." She smiles and I sink into my seat. What the hell was I thinking?

Fuck. Now how am I going to get out of this? Lynn pops into my head again. Maybe if I just explain the situation to her, she'll come with me out of pity. I mean, don't friends do things for each other like this? The thought of spending the night with Tommy or anyone else my mother wants to set me up with is enough to make me think about skipping Thanksgiving all together.

Chapter 9

Lynn

It's the middle of the day on a Friday when Sophie surprises me with some coffee and a sandwich from Cinnamon Roll Saviors. I haven't eaten all morning so I'm digging in before she can even sit down. I know it's not lady-like but fuck it, I need to eat.

"Wow, I'm glad I thought to bring you some food. Don't they feed you here?" Sophie jokes as she hops up on the tattooing table and takes a sip of her hot coffee.

"I forgot to eat breakfast because I was in a rush, so this visit is greatly appreciated." I smile between bites.

"Glad I could help. I was in the neighborhood after work and wanted to stop by; I hope that's okay," she says worriedly.

"You're always welcome to stop by," I assure her.

"Thank goodness, because I, well, I need to ask you something."

"Seems serious," I joke.

"Well..."

I brace myself for whatever she might say next. She wants to date, she wants to end this, she's moving to Canada, anything. I don't know her well enough to decipher her tone yet.

"So let me start by saying my family is super traditional."

"Okay..." I have zero clue where she's going with this.

"So I was at my parents' house for dinner last week, and they brought up my ex and how great he was. Which, no, he wasn't. But they loved him, and honestly that's why I stayed as long as I did."

"I get it, my parents are a little overbearing too." I think about the lie I told them about having a girlfriend, and I've been avoiding my mother's calls again.

"Yes, so she brought up Thanksgiving and how I should bring someone with me."

"Oh, is this like the exclusive talk? Because it's fine if you bring someone else, but I'd prefer if you get tested if you sleep with anyone else," I say quickly. Even though the thought of Sophie with anyone else is enough to kill me. I grind my teeth just thinking about her kissing or touching anyone that isn't me. I know I have no right, so I play it off like we're cool.

"Well, good to know where we stand, but no. I was sort of wondering if you'd come with me. It can be as platonic as you want it to be, but I can't show up to this thing alone."

"I thought you said your parents are super traditional," I point out. Wouldn't bringing a woman kind of be the opposite of what they're looking for?

"They are." She sighs. "And yes."

"So, why me?"

"Because I like hanging out with you, and I'm kind of the black sheep of the family, so if I can rile them up a little bit just by being myself, I kind of want to," she admits.

"Okay." I pause. Taking it all in. "Am I going as your friend then..."

"Well, I was hoping you wouldn't mind pretending to be

my girlfriend. Just to get my parents off my back. They want to set me up with this creepy man, and I know if I show up alone they'll invite him over." She frowns.

I think about it. I mean, what's one day of us acting like we're more than friends? It's not like anything is going on between us besides some really hot sex. We've hooked up a few times now, and it's great. Sure, she still isn't ready to go down on me, but we're building up to that. I'm still getting used to being with her, and she's getting used to being with a woman.

Just as I'm about to say yes, the thought of my parents pop into my head. This might just be the answer I was looking for.

"I can do it," I say, and she smiles from ear to ear. "But I need something from you, too."

"Sure, anything."

"I need you to pretend to be my girlfriend in front of my parents, too."

"Okay, but why?" She raises an eyebrow.

"I kind of lied and told them I was seeing someone so I wouldn't have to go home for the holidays," I admit.

"Oh. I get that."

"It's not like you have to meet them or anything. But maybe we can send them a holiday card together so it looks like I'm telling the truth."

"I can do that. I'm bomb at photoshop." She laughs.

"You have no idea how much you're saving me."

"No, trust me. You have no idea how much you're saving me." She smiles and stands. I put down my sandwich and she straddles me, her lips meeting mine.

She kisses me fiercely and passionately, our lips dancing as well as our tongues. I pull her close by her perfectly round ass, and she begins grinding on my lap. Sure, I don't have a dick but I'm not immune to a hot woman rubbing her body on mine. I'm about to lay her on the table and take her right now when I hear a knock at the door. It's a light one, meaning it's Addie telling me it's time for my next appointment.

"I'm sorry, but can we continue this later?" I ask hopefully.

"Yes, why don't you come over to my place this time?" she asks.

"Sounds good, shoot me an address." I grab one last lingering kiss before she goes, and then I say goodbye, watching her leave. Damn, she has one nice ass.

"Sorry, but your one o'clock is here, and I thought you'd want to know," Addie says with a half-smile.

"Of course." I force a smile back. I don't want Sophie to go, but I do need to get back to work. Kissing isn't going to pay the bills.

I PULL up to Sophie's apartment at eight o'clock. I managed to grab a quick shower before heading over and changed out of my work clothes. I have a bag of clothes with me just in case I stay over, but I leave it in my trunk. I don't want to be too presumptuous with an overnight bag in hand.

"Hey!" Sophie answers the door in just a T-shirt and a tiny pair of shorts despite the cold November weather.

"You're going to get sick, close the door!" I quickly rush inside.

"Eh, I'm fine." She waves me off. "It's nice to see you." She stands on her toes and wraps her arms around my neck, leaning in for a kiss.

"It's nice to see you again too," I murmur. I could get used to this, which is part of the problem; I'm becoming more and more attached to Sophie.

"We can watch a movie first or we can just go to my bedroom, I've been craving you." She bites down on her bottom lip.

"Let's go to your room," I say with a whisper.

"I bought something. I hope that's okay," she says quietly, taking my hand and leading me to her bedroom.

"I'm intrigued," I admit.

"It's a strap on. I know you said you have one. But I wanted a new one for just us."

"That's okay." I nod. I don't blame her for wanting a new one.

"It's pink, and bigger than I thought it would be." She pulls out the strap on from her nightstand, and it's complete with a black harness and an at least eight-inch lifelike dildo attached.

"It's about the same as mine, but it looks bigger because it's as big as it can get," I point out.

"That's true. Would you, would you use it on me? I really want to try it." She's nervous again, so I take it from her and nod.

"I'll go put it on, why don't you lie in the bed and try to relax."

"Okay." She nods and tells me the bathroom is just down the hall.

I find it and strip down to my panties. It's easier to leave them on to prevent chafing from the belt. I glance in the mirror and I'm a little impressed with how I look. I hope Sophie thinks the same of me. I take a deep breath and head back to her, where I find her completely naked on the bed, touching herself. Fuck if that isn't a sight to see.

"You told me to relax," she whispers innocently.

"Are you?"

"I am very relaxed now." She smiles, her hands not leaving her clit that she's rubbing small circles around.

"Fuck," I mutter and climb in the bed with her.

Pushing her hands away, she groans and I lean down to kiss her instead. I want to warm her up for this. She's already wet, I can feel it on my thigh, but I want her to be dripping before I slide inside her.

"Oh!" She gasps as I bend down to take her nipples in my mouth and tease her pussy at the same time. I push my thigh against her core, and she gasps out in pleasure.

"Mmm, I want you dripping, baby."

"I—I will be," she stutters out. I have that much control over her right now, and I love it.

I run two fingers through her pussy, soaking up all her juices and watching as she grows wetter and wetter as my mouth dips closer to her core. I kiss down on her hip bones, and she bucks her hips to bring my mouth closer to her. I slide my tongue across her clit ever so slightly, and she moans beautifully for me. Her legs spread wide, and I lick up all her juices, tasting her sweet pussy. I can tell she wants this, but I want to fuck her. I don't want her coming on my tongue just yet.

"Are you ready?" I ask her. Her body is more than ready but I just want to double check.

"Oh, yes." She nods and smiles.

I position myself between her thighs, holding up her legs, and she surprises me by folding them over by her head. Holy shit this woman is flexible. With that, I slide the tip in ever so slightly and she moans for me. I push in deeper and deeper, slowly watching her face as it twists in pleasure. She's loving every second of this being inside her. I'm dripping, my panties doing nothing to keep my arousal at bay. Maybe tonight she'll be more apt to help me. I don't want to push her, going down on a woman for the first time is a little scary, but fuck it feels so good.

I hold onto her legs, thrusting my hips to push the dildo deeper inside her until she's taking all of it. I watch as it slides in and out of her pussy. She's so tight that it grips it, her juices thankfully acting as lube while I fuck her. I push my hips back and forth, watching as Sophie screams out in pleasure.

"Oh my god! You feel so fucking good." She moans and her breathing is heavy. She's moving her hips like I'm not giving her enough so I begin to move even faster. Sophie is breathless under me as I take two fingers and start to play with her clit.

"Fuck! I'm so close, baby." I don't know where that came from but damn does it spur me on. I move my hips and my fingers even faster over her, and she's squirming. Her release is close, and I need to see her come for me.

"Come on, baby girl, you can do it. Come for me." I lean down and breathe against her lips. She never breaks eye contact with me as she begins to shudder her release. I watch as her body shivers and her eyes clamp closed when she just can't take it anymore.

"Oh, fuck! Baby, yes! Yes! Yes!" She screams out loud enough for neighbors to hear but I don't give a fuck. I made Sophie come that hard, and I want the world to know it.

Chapter 10

Sophie

I know I shouldn't be afraid but there's something nerve-racking about going down on a woman for the first time. It's not like I don't want to know what Lynn tastes like; it's my fear that I may not like it once I'm down there. And then what do you do? Just stop? I mean yeah, but that would really suck. I like doing everything else with Lynn, so I know I'm at least sort of into women. I just don't know *how much* I'm into women.

But tonight is the night. I've read up on articles of what not to do and what I should do. I talked to Delilah about it, who eased some of my nerves. And I'm with Lynn, the most understanding woman in the world. It's just a little more daunting than I'm making it out to be. I mean, it's just a vagina for fuck's sake.

Lynn takes off the strap on and puts it on my nightstand. But I look at her breasts, her body, and I know I want to do this now. Before I lose my nerve. So I start kissing her, our lips and tongues tangling together. Then I slide my legs over her body and straddle her, much like I had at work earlier today. I like being on top of her; it's fun. I dip my head down and take her nipples in my mouth, playing with the metal bar between my lips. Flicking it gently with my tongue. She moans lightly in my ear, and it pushes me on.

"I want to fuck you," I say, looking directly at her.

"Okay." She smiles and kisses me again once more before I slide my body down until I'm face-to-face with her pussy. No fucking pressure. I can see how wet she is through her thin cotton panties, a huge wet spot forming just for me.

"You don't have to if you're not ready," she reminds me. But I ignore her. I want this.

Instead, I play with the hem of her panties and slide them down her deliciously thick thighs. She kicks them to the side, and I look at her pussy. It's just me and her now. I'm still nervous, like what if I mess up and hurt her or I don't know what I'm doing and it feels bad for her? But I push those thoughts out of my mind and slowly inch forward.

Pushing my tongue out against her clit, I lick slowly. Her hips buck immediately, and her breathing changes. I guess I'm doing something right with a reaction like that. So I lick again, watching as her breathing gets heavier and her body bucks under my touch. It's addicting...being able to have that kind of power over someone with just my tongue. It's like when I gave a guy head, and I swear I could ask for anything in that moment and I'd get it.

Lynn looks down at me as I begin to lick her clit with more of a rhythm. I flatten my tongue and lick it, getting a taste of her as it dips between her folds. I follow the sounds she's making and when her hand goes to my hair, I know I'm on the right track. I begin sucking lightly on her clit, careful not to use any teeth, and she shivers. Her head falls back into the pillows, her dark hair all over the place. I push my hair out of the way when it starts to fall in my face.

Tying it back quickly with a hair tie, I go back to eating her pussy.

"Oh, baby girl," she calls out. I know I started the pet names, but I love that she calls me that. It makes me want her to come so fucking bad. I'm wet again, this time from the taste of her, from her moans and sounds.

"I love how you taste," I say quietly.

"Mmm." She leaves a hand on my head, pushing my face down gently to keep going.

I take her hint and use my fingers this time. Thinking about all the times she's made me come and how many fingers she usually uses. I slide two inside her pussy and curl them like I do when I'm fingering myself. She must love it because suddenly she's uttering a string of curse words and gripping my hair a little tighter than before.

"I'm coming! Oh! I'm coming!" She screams. I reach up to flick her nipples with my fingers, and she screams even louder. I'm afraid my neighbors might hear but I don't give a fuck in this moment. I want Lynn to keep coming and coming.

Once we're both cleaned up and spent from sex, we decide to take a shower. I don't think I've ever taken a shower with someone else before so I don't know what to expect. But as Lynn hands me a washcloth, I have an urge to wash her. I squirt some soap on the washcloth and begin wiping it over Lynn's breasts. She smiles and I look at how beautiful she is. My eyes find a small dimple on her cheek I've never noticed until now.

Lynn stands under the water and then begins to clean my back. She rubs it gently and then places kisses along my neck. I close my eyes, taking in all the smells of the soap, the feel of her fingers and lips on my skin, and how nice the hot water feels. This feels like a dream. We kiss until the water runs cold. Then, we head back to my room, and I change into pajamas while Lynn excuses herself to run to the car. We never really talked about her staying over, but we also never talked about her *not* staying over.

Lynn comes back with a small overnight bag and changes into some pajamas. Then we both climb into my bed and she wraps her arms around me, and everything else seems to fall right into place.

♡♡♡

IN THE MORNING, I'm the first to wake. But it's a hazard of mine from waking up so early during the week. I don't have any classes today, so I could sleep in, but I'm already awake. I turn on the Keurig machine and make myself some coffee and a slice of avocado toast. I slip back into bed next to Lynn and wait for her to wake up. For a while, I just lie in her arms, then I scroll on my phone for a bit.

It's around nine o'clock when Lynn finally wakes up. She turns and looks around, and I smile at her. I lean in to kiss her but she backs away quickly.

"I haven't brushed my teeth!" she exclaims, holding a hand over her mouth.

"Oh, I don't care about morning breath." I shrug.

"Well, I do." She shakes her head and jumps out of the bed to go brush her teeth, grabbing her toothbrush from her bag. I guess she had thought to bring everything just in case.

Five minutes later, she's back with a clean set of teeth and I finally get my minty kiss.

"Good morning."

"Good morning." She smiles. "Have you been awake long?"

"Yeah, I couldn't sleep again," I admit.

"You slept pretty well last night, Miss Snores McGee," she teases.

"What!? I do not snore." My eyes widen.

"You do, but it's cute as hell." She kisses my nose and climbs out of bed.

"Do you have anything to do today?"

"No work, if that's what you're asking."

"Do you want to stay and have brunch with me? We can grab something in town if you'd like."

"Like a date?" She raises an eyebrow at me.

"Like two friends having brunch after a night of hot sex," I say.

"Sure, let me get dressed." She picks up her bag and heads to the bathroom. I walk to my dresser and pick out a pink sweater dress and a pair of tights and boots. It's cold out today, and I don't want to be caught freezing my ass off.

"Ready?" Lynn comes back in black ripped jeans and a light green sweater that has some band logo on it. I make a mental note to ask her about that later.

We drive separately so Lynn can head home right after brunch. We decide to go to Cinnamon Roll Saviors, even though it's less of a brunch place and more of a breakfast place. The owner and barista, Lainey, is all too happy to see us when we walk in.

"Hey! I didn't know you two knew each other," she says, smiling. I'm sure Lainey knows everyone in town. Not that Seaside is big or anything.

"We go way back...to a few weeks ago," Lynn teases.

"Well, what can I get you two?"

"Two cinnamon rolls, a flat white coffee, and a Pumpkin spiced latte," Lynn orders for both of us. What has me more impressed is that she knows my coffee order. I try to pay her and she shoves my money away like it's on fire or something.

"Thank you," I mumble and take my coffee from Lainey.

"No problem." She winks and my knees go a little unsteady. What the hell was that about?

We sit down and wait for our cinnamon rolls, which are the best. No other cinnamon rolls compare. They're soft and warm and gooey with lots of frosting. It's barely a breakfast and more of a dessert but they are way too good to pass up. I'll dance off the calories later. I'm not too worried about it. The holidays are a time to gain a few extra pounds from all the good food.

"So, what are you up to today?" Lynn asks me while I make a fool of myself trying to eat the cinnamon roll without making a mess. I'm failing miserably, but at least I know I don't need to impress Lynn. She's seen me naked and acted like she wanted me more than anyone else ever had. She isn't going to judge me because I'm making a mess out of this cinnamon roll.

"I think I'm going to stop by the studio and check in on things. I also have to post some TikTok videos to my account today. So maybe I'll go live later," I say with a shrug. TikTok is a low stress job; I don't need to put too much thought into it.

"You still won't share this secret TikTok with me?" Lynn teases.

"Give me your phone." I roll my eyes. I've left her in the dark long enough. She hands me her phone, and I pull up TikTok, type in my username, and let her follow me.

She takes the phone back and starts looking at the videos. "Wow, you're insanely talented," she comments.

"You think?" I ask, fishing for a compliment. It isn't my usual style but hearing it from Lynn hits different. I really care what she thinks about me.

"Oh, I know so. You have so much talent." She smiles and I do too.

It's nice just hanging out with Lynn like this. No pressure to be naked or do anything, no pressure at all. I can be myself around her, and I love that. I've never clicked with someone this fast before—aside from Delilah. And that's different. This almost feels like she's some kind of soulmate of mine or something. I know it sounds crazy, but I think Lynn and I were meant to meet. Now that she's my fake girlfriend, I can't help but wonder what things would be like if she were my real girlfriend. But instead of thinking about it too much, I listen to Lynn talk about her next tattoo client and her excitement about it.

Chapter 11

Lynn

I brace myself for what's to come. Sophie has warned me how traditional her family can be. I've thought about backing out a few times but I don't want to leave her hanging. I know she needs me to come more than she lets on. Besides, it is practice for just in case I need to have her on a phone call with my family or something. My mom calls as I'm walking out the door, and I answer it for once, happy I have something positive to say.

"Well finally!" she says, frustrated. I have been ignoring her calls again lately.

"Sorry. I'm headed to my girlfriend's parents' house for Thanksgiving," I explain quickly and her tone changes dramatically.

"Oh, really!? That's so exciting! Are you bringing anything? I told you its rude to show up somewhere with nothing."

"I picked up a fresh baked pie after work today," I say. I had only gone in for a few hours but it was busy as hell. Everyone wanted to get a tattoo and get away from their families today.

"You didn't bake one? I suppose that'll do." She sighs. And

I take a deep breath. I'm not going to let her ruin my day before it has even started.

"Happy Thanksgiving, Mom. I'll have to call you later. I'm almost there," I lie. I have another ten minutes according to my GPS, but I want the silence to brace myself.

"Okay, okay! Have fun!" She hangs up before I can, and I take a few deep breaths to calm myself. I hate how riled up my mother's calls leave me.

I drive to Sophie's parents' house and the first thing I notice is the religious cross on her garage. What is Sophie having me walk into? I don't want to make any assumptions about her family but with the way she talks about them being traditional, I know my appearance is going to ruffle some feathers. I text Sophie that I'm here and then ring the doorbell.

"Hey," Sophie whispers as she steps outside and closes the door behind her. "Are you ready?"

"I think so," I say nervously. I'm more nervous about meeting her parents than I want to let on.

"You'll do great, and my brother will love you." She smiles and takes my free hand, rushing me into the house.

"Mom! Dad! My plus one is here!" Sophie announces loudly.

A middle-aged white woman with an apron on comes out from what I assume is the kitchen. She's smiling until she sees me. She looks me over not once, but twice, and then frowns at her daughter. Oh yeah, this is going to be an interesting night.

"Mom, this is my girlfriend, Lynn." Hearing her say it out loud does something to my stomach. I know it's all pretend, but what if we could be more?

I have to push those thoughts away for right now.

"Hi, it's so nice to meet you." I smile and hold out the pie I brought.

"That's so kind of you. Sophie, why don't you help me with

it in the kitchen? I need to have a word with you," her mother says sharply. I can only guess what her conversation is about.

"Make yourself at home," Sophie tells me before following her mother into the kitchen.

"Hey, I'm Montgomery, but everyone calls me Monty," a handsome older man says. This must be Sophie's brother; she's told me a lot about him and how close they were while growing up.

"Hey, it's nice to meet you." I smile again and hold out my hand. He shakes it firmly, and we make small talk while Sophie and her mom are in the kitchen. Her dad is nowhere to be seen but I see two little girls running over to greet us.

"Hi! I'm Jesse," she says, twirling her dress around in a circle. Her sister stands behind Monty and looks at me without saying anything.

"That's my sister, Jemma, but she doesn't like to talk to new people. She has anxiety. Do you have *anxiety*?" Jesse asks, pronouncing the word with emphasis on each letter.

"Nope, I do get nervous around new people sometimes though," I admit. I wave to Jemma, and Jesse looks between us.

"Well, I'm not shy. Did Sophie say she's your girlfriend? Does that mean like best friend?" Jesse asks going a mile a minute.

"Uh..." I look to Monty for help. I don't know how to explain that one to his kids.

"It means they go on dates and kiss sometimes, like how Daddy used to with Mommy," he explains, and I smile. It's nice that he's normalizing something to them instead of making it seem like such a huge thing.

"That's cool, can I have a girlfriend?" Jesse asks without skipping a beat.

"No, not until you're older." Monty chuckles.

"Okay!" Jesse shrugs and pulls Jemma away to go back to the game they were playing at their little table in the corner.

It's then that I see Sophie and Monty's dad. He's in the recliner, eyes steady on the football game, and he barely glances when Monty and I walk around him to sit down. I guess he's the quiet type. I don't blame him. If he has to keep up with his wife, he probably has his work cut out for him. She seems like she has an opinion on everything.

"Lynn, can I talk to you?" Sophie calls me, and I see the red rims around her eyes. She's on the verge of crying. *What the hell had her mother said to her?*

"Of course." I get up and follow her outside to the front porch.

"What happened?" I ask when we're alone.

"My mother said a lot of things about me being with a woman that I thought she might say. But hearing her say it is a lot worse," she says with a sigh.

"I'm sorry." I reach for her hand and pull her in for a hug. It lingers longer than I expect it too, and afterward, I'm left feeling more confused about my feelings for her.

"It's not your fault. I knew I was going to rattle her a bit."

"Do you want me to go? I understand if you do."

"No! I really don't," she says quickly.

"Okay, then I can stay." Whatever she needs, I'm here.

"Are you sure? I doubt she'll say anything to you but it's bound to be uncomfortable now." Sophie frowns.

"I can handle myself as long as you're okay. It's hard to hear those things from anyone, but I can't imagine it from your parents."

"Your parents know you're into women?"

"They do, and they've always been very accepting of it. They have more issues with me being a tattoo artist than being gay," I say with a shrug. It doesn't make any sense to me but what can I do?

"Well, I'm sorry about my mother. I don't know how my dad feels but he's always been a bit of a quiet man," she explains.

"You don't have to apologize for your parents. They aren't you. As long as you feel happy with whatever this is, then I do too," I admit, refraining from actually labeling us.

"I'm very happy." Sophie smiles and leans in to kiss me.

Our lips linger until we hear someone clear their throat behind us.

"Sorry, but Mom wanted me to tell you that dinner's ready," Monty says with a blush across his cheeks, similar to Sophie's.

"Coming!" Sophie calls back and we both giggle as Monty closes the door behind him.

"I think that's the first time he's caught me kissing someone else, he looked so embarrassed." Sophie laughs.

"He looked like he caught us doing more than kissing," I tease.

"Save that for later," she whispers, and she takes my hand before leading me back inside.

I know it would be easier to just head home, but I don't want to leave Sophie stranded. I can handle homophobic people, but what I can't do is leave Sophie to fend for herself. I mean, what kind of fake girlfriend would I be?

"Oh, Lynn I'm so glad you're still joining us," her mother says upon seeing me reenter the kitchen.

"I just couldn't stay away from your delicious cooking." I smile through my teeth.

"Well, please have a seat next to Sophie. We pulled out an extra chair for you." I can tell how hard she's trying to be fake so she doesn't come across as a bitch. At least she isn't being homophobic to my face.

I take a seat, low key looking for tacks or something to be on my seat. Not that she would, but hey, you never know what kind of antics people can get up to. Sophie's mom says grace, and I clasp my hands together like they do, sitting in silence. I'm not much of a religious person but I'm also not one to dismiss someone else's religion in their home. I take the time to notice that Sophie isn't saying grace either, she is just holding her head down.

"So, Lynn is it? What do you do for work?" her mother asks, and the table's focus is on me.

"I'm a tattoo artist, ma'am," I explain. Then I wonder if her mother knows how Sophie and I met. Not that it's my place to say anything.

"Oh." Her eyes widen in distaste, and she passes the peas to her husband.

"That's cool, do you have any tattoos?" Monty asks me.

"I do." I roll up my sleeves of my sweater dress to show them just a taste of some of my tattoos. Most of my body is covered at this point but they're still easy to cover up if need be.

"Wow!" Monty looks at them in appreciation.

"So, how exactly did you two meet then?" her mother asks, looking between us.

I take a large sip of water and look at Sophie who's paled a bit. But she rights herself and then looks at me.

"She was my tattoo artist when I went to get a tattoo," Sophie says proudly. I smile at her, loving that that is our story.

"A tattoo?!" Her mother doesn't hold back her surprise or distaste.

"No way!" Monty laughs.

"Yeah, I got one and I like it a lot, I'll probably be getting more," Sophie says with a shrug like it's no big deal.

"First you bring home a woman like it's an appropriate dinner *date,* and then you tell me you've defiled your body with a tattoo?!" Her mother is enraged and the table goes silent.

"Yes," Sophie says firmly, standing her ground.

"I don't think she's defiled anything," I say aloud.

"Don't you even—" Her mother is cut off by her father speaking.

"Margaret, I think that's enough."

"But—"

"Enough. Our daughter is happy, and that's what matters. None of the other stuff matters in the long run," he points out. I want to high five this man.

"I need some air." She stomps toward the kitchen, and we sit in silence, looking at the man who just gave us his approval.

"Thank you, Daddy." Sophie smiles at him.

"Just don't get any face tattoos; I think those are tacky," he says with a wink. How in the hell is this man married to that woman?

We all laugh and the rest of dinner is filled with small talk and ease. Her mother doesn't come back, and I don't think anyone misses her presence. I definitely don't. Sophie and I help clear the table after dinner, and her mother is still nowhere to be found. Sophie walks me out and we say goodnight.

"I'll come over later, okay? I want to check in with my mom and make sure she's not, like, going to kill me for tonight." She sighs.

"Of course. Just text me when you're on your way." I kiss her chastely and then head out.

Chapter 12

Sophie

"Did you really think it was appropriate to bring someone like *that* into my home? On a holiday no less?" My mother's words ring in my ears while I drive over to Lynn's house.

Our conversation replays in my head.

"*I didn't think you'd have this big of an issue with it,*" I lie. I knew she would but I also didn't think it would be any easier to come out to her. This was probably a shock to her, and I need her to see that it isn't just me trying to get a rise out of her.

"*Well, I do. It's unnatural.*" She scoffs.

"*It's more natural than all the other relationships I've been in, Mother. I can be myself with her and I'm happy—*"

"*Don't you try to tell me you're serious about someone like her.*"

"*I am.*" I know Lynn and I are only fake dating, but I can see it going somewhere if I admit to her that some of my feelings aren't so factious.

"*No daughter of mine is going to be so public about being with another woman in that way.*" She frowns. Tossing the pota-

toes in the bowl in front of her, she begins mashing them. She turns on the mixer so I can't get another word in.

Thankfully, over dinner, my dad stood up for me. Which meant more than I cared to admit. I tried talking to my mother after Lynn left but she wanted nothing to do with me. Shutting me out of the kitchen was enough but then I saw Lynn's pie in the garbage, and that was the last straw. I couldn't believe she wouldn't even eat the pie she brought. It was like she was afraid she was going to catch being gay. I knew how my mother felt about other people being gay, but I didn't know it would carry over to her own daughter.

The tears fall slowly from my cheeks as I drive through the snowy town. It's just starting to snow, and with the darkness, it isn't making it easy to drive. I sigh, wiping my eyes so I can see a bit better. I just need to make it to Lynn's and she will make it all better. I can't explain how, but I just know being with her will help.

I think about calling Delilah but I don't want to ruin their Thanksgiving. I'm sure she's enjoying being over her future in-laws house and getting to know the family even better than she already had. Part of me is jealous about how easy it is for her, but then again, I know how much she went through to get to this point. If anyone deserves a happy ending, it's her. I decide not to call her on my way over, and instead focus on driving in the dark snow. I hate that it gets pitch black at five o'clock now. I mean, no wonder people get depressed this time of year.

When I finally make it to Lynn's house, her lights are all on, and I see her through the window putting up a Christmas tree. *Already?* My family usually waits until at least December first but I guess she likes to get it over with early. I knock a few times, shivering in the cold, and Lynn opens the front door, letting me in and quickly shutting the door behind us.

"Hey." Lynn smiles and then looks me over. "Are you okay?"

"Of course," I lie. I don't know why I do, but I don't want to unload on Lynn.

"You're a terrible liar." She laughs. "What's going on? Was it your mom?"

I don't answer because the tears spill from my eyes instantly, and I can't stop them. Lynn pulls me in for a hug and she just lets me cry, holding me in her hallway while I let everything out.

"I knew she'd have some issues with it, but she's completely shutting me out." I sob into her chest.

"It's a big adjustment, she has to have a little time to get used to this new you." Lynn rubs my hair back and holds my face in her hands.

"I know, I just thought she might be more understanding if it was her own daughter. You know, someone she loves unconditionally. But now it feels like there's all kinds of conditions." I sigh.

"I know, I wish she did too. But maybe she'll come around eventually. Just give her a little time." Lynn caresses my cheek with her thumb, and I lean into it. She wipes away my tears and eventually they stop falling. Her words and arms make me feel a billion times better.

"Do you want to help me put up my tree?" Lynn asks as we walk into her living room.

"Umm... not really," I admit and she chuckles.

"Good answer. Why don't we stuff our faces with cookie dough and watch a shitty Christmas movie instead?"

"I'd love that." I smile.

"Perfect, do you want something to drink?"

"Can we have wine and cookie dough?" I ask.

"Hell yeah we can! I have the kind you like." She smiles and heads to the kitchen.

Lynn returns a few minutes later with two glasses of wine and the holiday Pillsbury cookie dough. The kind with the little trees on it, which happens to be my favorite kind of cookie dough.

"I love this kind," I say aloud.

"Who doesn't?" Lynn takes a piece and settles her wine glass down on the table next to her.

Furball appears out of nowhere and climbs on the couch, covering my feet with her body. I laugh and Lynn tries to shoo her away but she stays put.

"I don't mind her, she's like my personal foot warmer." I smile. I'm glad Furball is warming up to me.

"Whatever you say." Lynn rolls her eyes as she picks up the remote and looks for a movie.

We settle on *Christmas with the Kranks*, the Christmas movie with Tim Allen and Jamie Lee Curtis. It's a good one that keeps my attention focused on the movie instead of my shitty mother. We eat cookie dough and sip wine together. We're laughing and having a good time, enjoying the movie together. About halfway through the movie, Lynn wraps her arms around me and pulls me in for some snuggles. We put a warm blanket on us and lean into the couch, and she puts feet up on the coffee table. We're extra cozy, and I know I could fall asleep in her arms, but I don't. It's barely six o'clock and I want to see the end of this movie. But there's an ease about being in her arms that brings a calmness over me.

When it's over, we put on another and order in some pizza. It's cheesy and warm and delicious as we laugh over the stupid holiday movie. It's something I've never seen before but proves to be funny enough to keep my attention on it. When the credits roll on the second film, we slide directly into a third movie and I'm still snug in Lynn's arms.

She gets up at some point to make us some hot cocoa and grab some more cookie dough from the fridge. Then, she feeds Furball her dinner in the kitchen, and we go right back to watching another holiday movie.

"Another one?" she asks when this one is over, but my eyes are shutting and a yawn escapes my lips.

"I'm too tired," I admit. I got up early with my mother to help prepare Thanksgiving lunch. It's finally starting to catch up to me.

"Do you want to stay over?" Lynn asks, and I pause. I don't know why I hesitate; I'm going to say yes.

I pause because it's the first time I'm sleeping over without us being intimate beforehand. And I think she's picked up that I'm in no mood to have sex tonight. But she's still asking me to stay. It blurs the line on our friends with benefits arrangement. But if it's not bothering her, then I won't let it bother me.

"Yes, I'd love to." I nod. She takes my hand and walks me to her room. She hands me one of her T-shirts that I like to wear as a nightshirt, and I smile. We both change into pajamas and climb into her bed.

"Do you ever think about the moon?" I ask.

"What about the moon?" She looks at me, confused.

"Do you think it ever gets lonely up there?" I frown.

"I don't."

"You don't think it gets lonely or you don't think about the moon?"

"Both. I suppose if I thought anyone was lonely it would be the sun, because of how hot and bright it is. I wouldn't want to be friends with the sun."

"I love the sun." I smile. "Do you like the summer?"

"Nope. I hate the summer. Too bright and the worst time to

get tattoos because everyone is in the sun and chlorine and they fade ten times faster."

"Hmm." I contemplate what she's saying.

"I like the snow and the winter. Everyone is covered up and taking care of their tattoos, and it's a great time to get them. The holidays create stress, and you know what's a great stress relief? Getting tattooed," Lynn continues on.

"I can attest to that." I laugh.

"I can't believe we've only known each other a few weeks," Lynn whispers.

"Why?"

"It just feels like I've known you so much longer than that," she says with a shrug.

"I feel that way too. It just feels like I've always known you."

"Exactly." She smiles and I can tell there's more on her mind but I don't push. If she wants to share, she will.

"Will you be here in the morning?" she asks. I had a habit of leaving most mornings before she was up because I had classes to teach or I was so restless from getting up so early.

"I'll be here," I decide. I don't have any classes tomorrow, and I I'll work on not being so restless. Something that seems a bit easier when I'm in Lynn's arms.

"Good, I like waking up to you next to me," Lynn admits before biting down on her bottom lip. I know what she's saying without her even needing to say it. She likes having me here a little more than she probably should. I know what she's saying, because I feel the same way about her.

She closes her eyes, and I turn over, wiggling my ass against her and she chuckles. I can almost feel her shaking her head behind me. Lynn is quiet but she pulls my body against hers and leaves her arms wrapped around me. It's the way we always fall asleep, but I don't know, something about it feels more intimate tonight. Like there's more to us than just sex and we know it. I don't say anything and neither does she. I think we're both okay with whatever this is and whatever direction it's going in.

I close my eyes and will myself to fall asleep. Ignoring the thoughts of my mother and everything else that's happened today. I focus on Lynn instead. The good parts of us and how happy we make each other. I don't know where it's heading, but I know that whatever it is is enough to make me happy. So I focus on that as the wave of sleep rushes over me. I let myself yawn quietly, listening to the sounds of Lynn's soft sighs while she sleeps. I hear her heartbeat beating against my back while I let myself fall asleep. Just knowing she's there is enough to let my body relax and my mind find quiet.

Chapter 13

Lynn

It was rare for me to have a full day off but today was that day, and I planned on sleeping in until at least eleven. Sophie was supposed to come over by noon, and I wanted plenty of time to get ready. But it's barely ten a.m. when I hear a baby crying and a knock on my front door. *Who the hell is here? And where is the baby crying coming from?* As far as I know, no one in my apartment complex has any children. Not that I'm against kids, they're great. I just don't want any in my apartment at ten a.m. But I throw on my robe, go to the front door, and look through my peep hole. Standing in the doorway is my boss and friend, Reagan, holding her baby, Emmett. I open the door and look at her, confusion swelling inside of me.

"Bathroom! I SO have to pee!" she exclaims, running into my house.

"That way!" I point, and she nods. She stops to hand me the baby, and he looks at me with the same confused expression I must have on.

"What is going on?" I hold him out like he's stinky because, being realistic, this might be the first time I've ever held a baby. I have no clue what the hell I am doing, and I don't want to drop him. I walk into the living room and sit down, waiting for Reagan to be done so she can explain what she's doing here.

"Hey! Thank you." She scoops up baby Emmett and gives him a little kiss on his head and then sits across from me.

"Did you stop by just to use my bathroom? Because you're welcome any time, but I was sleeping."

"I know, I tried calling but you didn't answer." She frowns.

"So you decided to risk it and wake me up instead?" My eyes widen.

"Well, yes. But also, there's a delicate conversation that I need to have with you but you're always working, and I didn't want to have this conversation at the shop."

"Are you firing me? Because I think that's illegal to do that in someone's house," I point out.

"What? No! Shush." She waves me off with her tattooed hand. She has more tattoos than I do at this point, although it's been a good year since she's gotten any new ones.

"Then what?" I prompt.

"I'm looking to take back some time at the shop so I can be there for my kids more. With that, I'd like to ask if you'd like to take on some more hours and responsibilities."

"Oh," I say because I don't know what to say. Do I want to work more and take on more at the shop? I'm pretty satisfied with what I'm doing already. Do I want to make my job more complicated than it already is?

"I'm looking to make you a partner of Rainy Day Tattoos. You're talented and smart, and I trust you. It would require you to be the manager when I'm not around, but other than that, it's your normal responsibilities. You'd just have a higher ranking than the rest of the shop."

"Why me?" I ask curiously.

"Look, you've worked here the longest. You've made a lot of clients become returning clients, and your Medusa tattoos have really taken off and become great press for the shop. I know that's not why you started it, but you're helping so many survivors out there, and I want you to be able to help more. Maybe offering a day every so often where all the artists tattoo Medusa for free—or whatever the client can pay," Reagan explains. Baby Emmett bounces on her lap, sucking on his fingers, and I look at her in shock. I had no idea Reagan thought so highly of me that she'd be willing to make me partner of the shop.

"Wow. I mean this is an incredible opportunity..."

"But you need to think about it, I get it. Just please don't say no without thinking about it?"

"Okay. I can promise that." I nod.

"Are you doing okay otherwise? Whatever happened with that girl you were texting a few weeks ago?"

"She's actually my, uh, kind of girlfriend now, I think." I don't know what to tell Reagan. She's not someone I usually have to lie to, but it is a small town, and things get around.

"You are! What's her name again?"

"Sophie." I smile.

"Oh! She owns the dance studio with my sister-in-law to be. She's so sweet, my daughter takes a class with her there." She smiles, putting a face to the name. I'm glad I lied about her being my girlfriend. I don't want it getting back to anyone that we're just faking it.

"That's awesome, I didn't realize you two knew each other."

"Well, Seaside is a small town." She laughs and I nod. That's exactly what I thought.

"So, with me stepping up does this mean you won't be tattooing as much?" I ask, changing the subject.

"Yeah, for now at least. I want to spend more time with the kids while they're still young. Plus we want to have more while we still can," she explains.

"Gotcha," I add.

"I should let you go, I'm sure you want to sleep," she says, standing up as I glance at the clock. They've been here an hour already? It's almost time for Sophie to get here.

"I'll definitely think about what we talked about." I smile.

"Please do. Just consider it to be a great step for your future. Even if you say no, I'd love to keep you on with your regular hours, and nothing will change. You're an amazing asset to the shop, and I know everyone agrees with me."

"Thank you." I smile. I didn't know how much I was appreciated until she was saying it, and it's really great to hear.

Chapter 14

Sophie

I show up to Lynn's house with a variety of options for me to wear. I don't know what kind of vibe she's going for, but I wanted to come prepared. I have a backpack full of clothes that I spent the morning picking out. Lynn had said to come over around noon, and I'm more than ready. I knock on her door, and I'm shocked to find Reagan on the other side of the door. She's Delilah's sister-in-law (to be). But what is she doing at Lynn's house?

"Oh! Hi, Sophie! Bye, Lynn!" Reagan smiles and excuses herself with her baby in tow.

"Hey, sorry. Come on in." Lynn looks stressed by Reagan's visit, but I wait until the door is shut to ask if she's okay.

"Yeah, Reagan just wanted..." Her voice trails off. "You look cute." She kisses me chastely, and I frown at her. I want her to finish her sentence.

"Sorry, she was asking if I had any interest in becoming a partner of Rainy Day Tattoos."

"What?! Seriously?!" I exclaim. That's so exciting.

"Yeah, but I don't know." Lynn shrugs.

"What do you mean you don't know?" I ask.

"Well, I don't know. It's a big adjustment and a lot to consider." She sighs. It's then I realize she's still in her pajamas and a robe. I guess Reagan's visit was of the surprise kind.

"What's to consider?"

"Well, I'd be manager when she's not around, and I'm not the best at telling people what to do. But on the opposing side, she said she'd let me do a Medusa event at the shop and get the other artists to help."

"What's a Medusa event?" I look at her, confused.

"So, sexual assault survivors often get the Medusa tattoo as a symbol of what they've overcome. I offer free Medusa tattoos to anyone who asks for one. No questions asked, no money or anything. It's my way of helping those who have been hurt," she explains.

"B-but you have one..." I think about the one on her shoulder.

"I do." She nods. I reach for her hands, and I realize how little I know about her. I thought I was falling for her but I realize now that we've only scratched the surface when it comes to what we know about each other.

"I'm sorry."

"Don't be. It was a long time ago, I went to therapy and talked about it there. I don't like it to affect my personal life now. But it's something important to me, and I help lots of survivors get their control and power back by tattooing it on their skin."

"So, a Medusa event would be something incredibly special and important to you."

"Yes, which I think is why she used that as a selling point with me."

"I think you should do it. I know you didn't ask, and maybe I'm overstepping, but I think you should. She believes in you, and you'd have the power to help so many new survivors if you made this a yearly event. It would bring so much good to their lives." I squeeze her hands in mine lightly, and she looks up at me.

"You're right."

"Wow, I don't hear that too often," I tease.

"I'm serious. I'm nervous about it, but it's all the right reasons I should do it. Who cares if I have to tell people what to do sometimes? It'll be worth it if we can do something for the greater good."

"I'm so proud of you." I lean over and straddle Lynn's lap. Just talking about her doing something so amazing makes me want to praise her. Show her how much I care about making her happy.

"Oh, yeah?" she mutters. My cheeks darken as I lower myself on her lap, and I can feel her zipper against my clit through my leggings. They're too damn thin for their own good.

"Yeah," I mumble back. I don't know why I'm suddenly nervous, like I haven't done this before.

"I want you," she whispers against my neck. Her hand runs down my back and grips my ass tightly.

"I want you more," I say with a heavy breath. My mouth is dry, and I can feel how badly we need each other in this moment. Something about our priorities has changed instantly. We need each other now.

"I have a surprise for you in the bedroom," Lynn says quietly.

"I don't think I can wait that long," I say, pulling off my sweater. Her eyes graze over my perky tits, and I blush again. I love it when the attention is on me.

"I think you can." Her eyebrows wiggle, and I bite down on my bottom lip. She's going to drive me crazy. She scoops me up with my legs around her waist and carries me down the hall to her bedroom. I'm kissing her neck the whole time, teasing her with my tongue, so when she drops me to the bed, I sigh.

"You said you wanted to try new things, right?" she asks, walking to her dresser.

"Yes..." I say cautiously. What does she have in mind?

"I bought some rope, and I thought we could practice my rope tying skills."

"You know how to tie me up..." My jaw drops.

"I do. I've only practiced with one other partner, but I'd like to try on you. If you trust me."

"Yes!" I exclaim. I have always wondered about being tied up, but there was never a man I was with that knew what he was doing, nor that I wanted to try it with. I mean, there has to be enough trust between us, and I never had that with my exes.

"Okay, lie down on the bed," she commands and strips down to her own panties, no bra. I grow wet just at the sight of her, but then she's holding bright pink rope, and I might melt.

Lynn takes the rope, does a series of twists and turns with it to begin, and then cuffs it around one of my wrists. She makes sure it's not too tight and then ties it to the bedpost before starting on the other side. Once I'm tied with both wrists to the bedpost, she stands at the edge of the bed and smirks at me. Just knowing I'm tied up and can't move has me wet in unimaginable ways.

"Fuck you look so good tied up to my bed, baby girl," she whispers.

"I'm so wet for you, baby." I whimper, twisting my legs together to relieve some of the ache I'm feeling.

"Oh, I'll have to do something about that, now won't we?" She smirks.

Walking alongside the bed, she stops at her nightstand and pulls out something purple. It's a lavender-ish looking vibrator of sorts. Oh, is she going to use this on me while I'm tied up?

Fuck yes. But she tosses it to the side and then climbs on the bed to straddle me.

"I can't tell you how bad I want you, baby girl," she says, but before I can reply, she crushes her lips over mine. Slipping her tongue in my mouth, I can feel all of her wetness on my thigh seeping from her thin panties.

"Mmm," I moan against her lips. I can feel how bad she wants this.

"Oh, baby girl, you feel so fucking good."

Before I can speak, she runs two fingers over my panties and begins circling my clit through them. I'm breathing heavy, unable to speak as she teases me. I move my hands to try and touch her, but I can't. I'm only met with resistance against the rope.

"Oh, you want to touch me don't you, baby girl?"

"Y-yes," I stutter.

"You better be a good girl and come for me then." She lightly taps my pussy with her hand, and I whimper under her touch.

"I'll be so good," I answer.

Lynn smiles at me and dips down to pull my panties achingly slow down my legs. It's like she's getting off on torturing me. I don't blame her, but fuck, this is annoying. Like the kind of annoying I don't truly mind, but it's still annoying.

Lynn runs her fingers through my folds. Her fingers glisten with my juices, and she surprises me by dragging them to my mouth.

"Open wide," she whispers, and I do, sucking off every last drop of me from her fingers. She fucking giggles. I can't blame her for what she's doing to me. She is definitely getting off on this. Meanwhile, I'm aching from her limited touches.

"Please, baby," I beg, and she smiles. Kissing me lightly, she

Only for the Holidays

reaches next to us for the toy again, and she turns it on this time.

She presses it to my clit, and I gasp. She presses the button again twice more, and the intensity of the vibration increases. Only, it isn't really vibrating...it's more like...sucking? Holy shit, she has one of those clit sucking vibrators.

"Oh!" I call out as she turns it up one last time to the highest it can go. It feels delicious.

"You like that, baby girl?" She smirks as she holds the toy in place.

"I do," I say breathlessly, as the sensation continues on my clit.

Her hands reach for my breasts, freeing them of my bra. She takes each nipple in her mouth, hardening them as she sucks on them. Her hands work their way down my stomach and inside my pussy. She uses two fingers, and I feel so incredibly full from them. With the sensation of the clit sucker on me and her fingers curling inside me, I feel close as hell. I move against the rope, trying to touch Lynn, desperate for her touch and only growing wetter when I can't have it.

"Oh, baby. I love seeing you like this. You tied to my bed is such a beautiful sight," she murmurs.

"I'm so close, baby," I moan.

"Then I want you to scream my name for me," she commands. I nod, feeling the orgasm on the rise as her fingers pump in and out of me with precision. The toy sits steadily on my clit. Suddenly the sensation is too much, and I'm seeing fucking stars. My pussy explodes, and I'm squirting all over Lynn's hand. I'm orgasming at the same time, and I've never felt so damn good in my whole life.

"Oh, Lynn!" I scream at the last second as I writhe in pleasure.

"That's my girl," she murmurs as she unties me from the

bed. I wrap my arms around her and pull her in for a deep kiss. I want her to know I'm every bit of hers as she is mine. My legs wrap around her waist, and I can't stop myself from touching her. I didn't realize how depraved I would feel until I couldn't touch her.

I push her down onto the bed and crawl between her thighs. Before she can speak, I'm pushing her panties to the side and devouring her. I lick and suck and run my tongue along and inside her folds, unable to get enough of her. I want every last drop of her. She moans under my touch as my nose brushes against her clit. So I take my thumb and brush it against her clit again, this time with more intention and she moans harder. I want to make her come for me, show her how good it feels. I slide three fingers inside her wet, dripping pussy, and she gasps.

"Fuck!" she mutters, but I don't let up. My tongue flicks across her clit with lightning speed as my hand works overtime in her pussy.

Reaching up with my spare hand, I play with her nipple rings. Flicking the metal bar with my fingers, I watch the reactions I get out of her. She's soaked and close to coming. I can feel her fingers tightening around me, and all I want is for her to let go and come for me. I push my fingers inside her harder and harder until she's shuttering and moaning for me.

"Oh, Sophie! Oh, baby girl! Oh, fuck!" She gasps out and cries into her sheets, gripping them for dear life. I don't let up until she's pushing my hand away, and still, I get in one last lick of her pussy before I pull away. She's addicting, and I want to soak up every moment I have with her.

Chapter 15

Lynn

"You're too fucking sexy looking like that," I tell Sophie as she saunters out of the bathroom in just a towel. We'd had sex a few more times and once the sheets were soaked and we were exhausted, we decided to take a shower. It ended up with us having sex again, and then the shower running cold on us. It isn't our fault we can't keep our hands off each other.

"I need to change the sheets again, can you grab a fresh set from the dryer?" I call out to Sophie.

"Of course." She kisses me softly, lingering just long enough to tease me before running off to the laundry room down the hall, completely naked. I take a moment to stare at her ass and watch as she shimmies down the hall.

I grab a fresh T-shirt for her to wear and a pair of pajamas for me, then I change into them and toss my towel aside for the laundry. I take the old sheets off the bed and toss them in a pile as Sophie comes back with the new sheets. This set is black and smells like lavender, fresh from the dryer. I wouldn't mind falling back asleep in these sheets.

I'm about to ask Sophie if she's up for a nap when I hear a knock at my front door. What is it with unexpected visitors today? It hasn't been too long since Reagan left, just a few hours, so maybe she forgot something?

"Get dressed, I'll check it out." I kiss Sophie's head and pick up my hairbrush to brush out my dark curls while I answer the door.

"Hell—Mom?" I open the front door and standing before me is none other than my mother.

"Hi sweetheart!" She throws her arms around me like it's a normal thing to show up on my doorstep unannounced.

"W-what are you doing here?" I stutter in complete shock as she invites herself in. My dad trails in behind her.

"I need a reason to come and visit my daughter during the holidays?" She waves me off like I'm crazy, and I close the door behind them. My brain latches onto Sophie and how this was not at all how I expected her to meet my parents. Hell, I didn't expect them to ever meet.

"I thought you knew I was working a lot."

"I did, but I took a chance! You're not working today clearly." She glances over my pajama clad body.

"No, but I—"

"Hi! You must be Lynn's mom and dad," Sophie says as she walks out of the room. She's dressed in a completely different outfit. It's a brand new holiday sweater, a pair of leggings, and bright, fluffy socks I've never seen before. It's like she's the epitome of pink Christmas right now.

"Oh my gosh! Is this the famous girlfriend?" My mom gasps and stands with a big smile across her face.

"Mom, Dad, this is my girlfriend, Sophie," I say quietly. This is a bit more complicated than we talked about, but I guess she's just rolling with it. I'll have to thank her for that later.

"Sophie, you are so pretty!" my mom gushes, touching her blonde hair.

"Thank you, Miss..." It occurs to both of us that we've never talked about last names. I've been sleeping with her for weeks, and we don't even know each other's last names. I try not to think too hard about that.

"Please, call me Christie." She waves her off like they're old friends and embraces her for a long hug. Thankfully, Sophie embraces her back with a large smile.

"Lynn, what is up with your tree?!" My mother's focus shifts to the half decorated tree in the corner of my living room. The top part of the tree isn't even connected fully.

"I was decorating it, and I got, umm, distracted?" I frown. I can't exactly tell my mother what I was distracted doing. Sophie blushes a deep red as she looks at the tree, and I hope my parents don't notice.

"Well, maybe we should all put it up then. I brought some lunch, and I was hoping Sophie would be here, but since she appears to have stayed here I can assume things are going well between you two?" My mother has always been too much of a detective to hide things from. It doesn't help that we're both sporting wet hair from the shower we just took.

"Things are going great, Mother." I force a smile to please her.

"Why don't we dig into some of the lovely lunch you brought, and I can put on some holiday music," Sophie suggests. "Any requests?"

"I have an old favorite," my dad chimes in.

"I'm sure my Spotify has it! What's it called?" Sophie picks up her phone.

"'Christmas Wrapping' by the Waitresses."

"Stop it! That's my favorite Christmas song!" Sophie exclaims, and I smile at her. Knowing how genuine her reaction is and how happy I am for her and my dad to have something to bond over.

"It's a classic." He smiles.

Sophie fills the air with music as my mom sets up lunch in the dining room. Even Furball makes an appearance to say hello to my parents. My dad helps me put the tree together, and I grab all my boxes of ornaments from the storage closet. My mom and Sophie are in the dining room, sipping wine and eating finger foods. They're chatting about God knows what, but I don't feel as stressed as I normally would. Sophie fits in here; it's almost like she's part of the family. She makes my parents go easier on me, and that's a gift in itself. I'll definitely be making things up to her later. In any way she wants.

"You look good, Lynn." My dad squeezes my arm, snapping me back to the present.

"Thanks, Dad."

"I mean it. Your mother worries, but it's nice to see you with someone who makes you so happy. There's a calmness about you that only comes when you're in love."

"Oh, I'm not—" I try to tell him I'm not in love with Sophie. I mean, I barely know her. I like her, and sure, maybe I want things to be more than they are, but I don't think that means I love her.

"I won't tell." My dad winks and puts a finger to his lips, telling me to shush just as Sophie walks over.

"Okay! What can I do? I love decorating."

"You do?" I look at her, surprised.

"Okay, no I don't. But your mom is right, this tree is too sad to look at anymore." She laughs.

"You can hang the garland around the room, but not too low because Furball likes to get ahold of it." I hand her a box of garland.

Sophie carries it to the dining room and starts hanging it

with the help of my dad. So my mom takes the opportunity to pull me aside. Sipping on her glass of wine, she looks me over and sighs. Oh no, here she goes. And I thought we were having such a nice time.

"You know, it's going to sound crazy. But I thought Sophie wasn't real," my mom says as I choke on the wine I'm sipping.

"W-what?" I look at her with panicked eyes. Had she seen through our facade?

"You told me about her out of nowhere. I thought you'd made up a girlfriend that didn't really exist. So, I'm sorry for thinking that. It's so nice to see the two of you together for real." She smiles and rubs my shoulder gently.

"Thank you, I think?" I furrow my brows together.

"It's really nice seeing you have someone for the holidays. I just never want you to be alone this time of year."

"I know, but even if I was, I'd be okay," I point out.

"Oh, I'm not worried about that. Of course you'd be okay. But you deserve to have someone look at you the way Sophie does." She smiles. Before I can say anything, Sophie and my dad are singing along to "Rockin' Around the Christmas Tree," and my mom is laughing up a storm.

I never really thought about it much. I always assumed my mother wanted me to be paired up was because of grandkids and not being okay being alone. But her saying she knew I'd be okay on my own? That meant more than I could really explain to her. It's like she believes in me being on my own and bringing myself happiness. I'm still not ready to give her grandkids, but for the first time, it doesn't feel like she's asking for them. She's just happy that I'm happy—which might be a first for us.

Sophie, my parents, and I end up having pizza for dinner and watching *A Christmas Story* on the couch after decorating. My dad naps through almost the entire movie, and my mom doesn't make a sound to wake him. It's sweet seeing them together all cuddly like this. It reminds me of Sophie and me. We fell into our natural spots on the couch, with Furball of course on Sophie's feet and a blanket keeping us warm.

"Well, we better hit the road. I have to get us back before the sunrise. Your sister has the kiddos in a play at the nursery school," my dad says, standing up and stretching. It's like he's pretending like he wasn't just napping for the last hour and a half.

"Ooo, take videos! I'd love to see that," Sophie gushes.

"Of course, dear. Here, give me your number and I'll send you the videos." My mom hands her the phone, and Sophie looks up at me expectantly. I know what she's asking: *Is this okay?* I nod silently and she smiles, putting her phone number in.

I get her worry but I don't think it'll hurt to have my mom and Sophie get to know each other a little bit better. I'm still conflicted about what my dad had said about us earlier, and I know I need some time to think everything over. I'll have to talk to Sophie about where this is going and what we're doing. Especially before I get too in my head about something that probably doesn't mean anything.

"Bye, Mom." I hug her tightly, and she kisses my cheek.

"Bye, Dad." I hug him, and he kisses my forehead, his beard tickling my head.

"Bye, Sophie, hopefully we'll see you soon!" my mom adds before shutting the door behind them.

"Whew!" Sophie says, and I look at her go from smiling to exhaustion in two seconds flat.

"You okay?" I ask.

"Oh, yeah, I just wasn't planning on being anyone's pretend girlfriend for the day. How'd I do? Did I play the part okay?" She smiles.

Of course she was just playing a part. How could I be so stupid to think there was something more here? I mean, we've talked about this already, and this is a temporary situation—something only for the holidays. I shouldn't think too much into this. I don't know why I let a few stupid comments go to my head. I sigh and realize Sophie's still waiting for a response from me.

"You did great, very believable." I force a smile.

"Thanks. It's easy to do when you have such a great girlfriend." She winks at me, and I ignore the ping in my stomach. I need to let go of this crush, or whatever it is that's getting my feelings all mixed up. I need to go back to just being her friend —with benefits of course. I turn off the thought of us being anything more than friends...

No matter how much my feelings for Sophie are still there.

Chapter 16

Sophie

"Do you want to stay?" Lynn asks shortly after her parents leave.

I'm torn as I look at her. As much as I want to stay, I know I probably shouldn't. So I shake my head and grab my stuff instead, watching as her head falls slightly in disappointment, and I feel just as bad as she does.

"I'll catch you tomorrow night?" I ask hopefully.

"Of course." She kisses me slowly and our lips linger longer than they should.

I head to my car just as the snow starts falling, and I immediately drive over to Delilah's house. I need to see my best friend today. And maybe squish those adorable babies of hers, too. Just seeing them in photos isn't enough for this auntie. When I pull up to her and Ryan's house, she answers the door with one twin on her hip and a yawn.

"Oh my gosh, did we have plans that I forgot about?!" Delilah asks with her eyes widening.

"No, no. It's an impromptu visit. Those are still okay, right?"

"Of course, come on in. Be warned, the place is a mess," she says with a sigh. I don't know what I expect, but it's not for the place to look like this. There are clothes and toys everywhere. It's like the house has thrown up on itself or something.

"Wow," I utter accidentally.

"I warned you." Delilah frowns. "Autumn hasn't been sleeping because she's teething so she's been keeping the rest of us up."

"Isn't it early for her to be teething?!" I ask, surprised.

"Yes, yes it is. But I guess we got an overachiever here," she says, pointing to the baby in her arms.

"Can I hold her?"

"She'll chew on everything if you let her, so just be careful," she warns before handing her to me.

"Hi, sweet baby," I murmur. She's so soft and sweet. It's like she makes all of my problems disappear.

"So, why are you here? Surely it isn't to hold my baby and see my messy house."

"Oh, I wanted to talk to you about Lynn," I explain.

"Go for it. I'm too tired to clean up this mess so my ears are all yours." She yawns.

"Where's Ryan?" I ask, suddenly remembering him.

"He's napping with Olivia; he's the only one who can get her down," she says with a shrug.

"Oh okay." I nod. "So I think I might be falling for Lynn."

"Yeah, that happens when you're pretending to be with someone." She laughs, referencing her life now. She had pretended to be engaged to Ryan before they were even dating.

"Well, I didn't expect it, and I surely didn't expect to meet her parents today."

"Oh, yeah that's always a tough one. Especially if they like you too, which I'm sure they did."

"They did." I groan. I hadn't expected to like them so much too.

"So what's the harm in liking this woman?" she asks, confused.

"It's not that I can't like her, it's that we said this was only friends with benefits. I'm not the girl that goes and gets feelings from that. I've always been able to separate feelings from sex. So why can't I do that with her?"

"Because maybe you're actually falling for her," Delilah points out.

"But why her? It feels like she's the one person I can't have so of course I have to fall for her. I mean, she only wants to be friends with me so why am I even acting like it's an option to have anything more?"

"Are you sure?"

"What?"

"Are you sure that's how she feels? Maybe she's having the same crisis with her best friend."

"I—"

"Look, all I'm saying is don't close the door on something until you're sure that you have to. You don't want to miss out on the possibility of something good. You deserve to have something good." She smiles.

"Thanks, I guess you're right. I just don't want to talk to her and end whatever we have going on. Because the rest of it is so good—I mean *deliriously* good."

"We get it, you're having great sex." Delilah rolls her eyes jokingly.

"When are you like able to again?" I ask.

"We got the green light this week, but we're both too exhausted to even think twice about it. We'd both rather get some sleep than anything." She laughs.

I look at Autumn who's taken to eating the side of my shirt

between her fingers. She seems to be happy so I don't mind. I can always wash my shirt later.

"Why don't you go nap with them, I can watch Autumn for a while and then you can feel like a person again," I suggest.

"Really? Are you sure?" Her eyes light up.

"I'm positive. Just tell me where her bottles are in case she gets hungry."

"I just pumped so there's some in the fridge, I seriously appreciate this Soph." She squeezes my arm lightly.

"Please, it's part of my auntie duties to take care of her. I love her." I smile down at her.

"I'll only be an hour, I swear."

"Take your time. I have nowhere to be." I wave her off.

She runs off to the bedroom and I look at Autumn.

"We can handle this, right?"

"Goo-bleh" Autumn mutters, and I take that as an agreement.

I pick her up and walk over to the fridge. I grab one of the frozen teething toys I assumed they had and hand it to Autumn. She takes it greedily from my hands, and I'm able to place her in the play yard. I thought she might complain but she just lies there looking at the toys above her and playing with her feet. Man, they are so cute and easy going at this age.

"I'm going to help out mama and daddy okay? So if you help me by staying in there, then I can clean up just a bit," I tell her. She mutters some baby language back at me, and I laugh.

I pick up all the baby clothes and blankets strewn about, making a pile for the laundry. Then I put all the toys away in their toy box and look for the vacuum. Autumn makes googling sounds when I use it so that must mean she likes it, I mean, she isn't crying. After a while her teething toy goes warm so I grab her a second one, trading it out, and she's content again.

Then I move her yard to the kitchen, so I can do some

dishes and clean up the counters. Wiping them all down and dancing around the kitchen, I see Autumn's eyes on me. When I'm all done, I take her out of the play yard and reward her with a bottle from the fridge. She's just starting to get fussy, and her diaper is still clean, thankfully. I've had enough of diaper changes with my own nieces.

"Whoa," Ryan's voice startles me. Looking up from the couch, I see him walking into the living room shirtless, holding baby Olivia. "Did we get robbed or did someone clean this place up?"

"I just did a little cleaning." I laugh.

"Oh, shit, Sophie. I'm sorry. Let me go grab a shirt."

"Ryan, it's your house, and trust me it doesn't do much for me these days. So just do whatever you're comfortable with," I tease.

"Oh yeah. I heard you've been more into the vagina monologues these days," he teases.

"I heard you haven't been," I tease back.

He stares me down. "I'll let that one go because I forgot this place had wooden floors, and I missed looking at them."

"Is Delilah still sleeping?"

"I didn't see her in our room, but maybe she's in the guest room," he says. "I came to give Olivia a bottle."

"There's a fresh one in the fridge; she pumped before she went to nap," I explain.

"Perfect." He grabs one and then takes a seat on the couch next to me. Autumn is almost done with her bottle so I look down at her smiling chubby cheeks.

"She's so precious."

"I know, I can't believe they're mine." He smiles proudly. "But seriously, Sophie, thank you for cleaning up. You didn't need to do that."

"I know, but Delilah looked like she needed some help.

Only for the Holidays

And I remember my brother raising twins quite well. He was always so thankful when we came over, but he said besides holding them that cleaning or doing a chore made such a difference for them."

"It really does, Dee is going to be so happy." He smiles.

"You'll have to tell me how that goes, because I do have to get going. I forgot I need to give my brother a call back tonight. But are you okay with the two of them?"

"I am! Just put Autumn in her bouncy seat. Do you mind burping her first?"

"Of course." I sit Autumn up on my shoulder and tap lightly on her back until I hear a string of small burps.

"Perfect, baby." I kiss her forehead and she scrunches her nose up at me.

"Bye, baby." I kiss Olivia's head and then wave goodbye to Ryan.

"Thanks again," he adds.

"Don't worry about it. I'll be back soon, just call if you guys need anything."

I leave their house feeling less clarity about my problems, but more clarity about my family issues. It's hard to imagine my life without my mother, but I've skipped the last few Sunday dinners. I don't want to be around anyone who doesn't understand my relationship with Lynn—real or not.

I grab my phone and call back my brother. I'd been avoiding his calls, too, fearful he'd tell me to come back to Sunday dinners or my mother had secretly gotten through to him.

"Well, would you look who it is," Monty teases from the other end.

"Oh, shush. You can't even see me."

"Which is good because I'd be kicking your ass for not picking up the phone."

"I was busy," I lie. It's not even a good lie, but it slips out too easily.

"Liar." He laughs. "Look, I know what happened with Mom wasn't easy..."

"Easy? She basically told me my relationship was a joke. She doesn't respect me, Monty. Or you, for that matter. She thinks she controls us, and it's ridiculous."

"I know, but she is *family*."

"No, Monty. Don't give me that bullshit about *family*. If she was truly family then love is unconditional. And she'd love me no matter what."

"You're right."

"I know." I laugh and he laughs too.

"Just tell me you'll come stop by and see the girls soon? Because they've been asking about you."

"Of course. I wouldn't miss seeing my favorite nieces." I smile. "Although now they have some competition since I have two sets of twin nieces."

"Oh, no. I'll have to let them know you're cheating on them."

"No, never. Although I was just with the other twins." I laugh.

"How's Delilah doing? Being a twin mom can be rough." What he's really saying isn't lost on me. His wife had left because she thought being a twin mom was too hard and couldn't be around to do it anymore. So I know his checking in on Delilah is more about making sure what happened to Jesse and Jemma doesn't happen again to her girls.

"She's doing good, I was just over there to help. I cleaned up and helped as much as I could," I explain.

"Good, I'm glad she has you." I want to tell Monty that it's different...that it's not his fault that his wife left, but I know

Only for the Holidays

how he feels about it. I don't blame him. His wife's postpartum depression also had a lot to do with it, in my opinion.

"I'm almost home, but I'll call you this week, okay?"

"Yes, please do." We hang up, and as I'm pulling into the driveway, I realize I've driven myself back to Lynn's house. Maybe subconscious or not, I called her house my home. I drove myself back here, and I still don't know how I feel about her. What the hell does that even mean?

Chapter 17

Lynn

I'm surprised when I see Sophie knocking at my door a few hours after she said she had to go. I didn't blame her for leaving, although it was disappointing. We've spent a lot of time together recently. I figured she wanted some alone time, and I could use the alone time too. I've become so entangled in Sophie lately that I've barely spent any time by myself. Before she knocked I was sitting on my couch, drawing up tattoos for an upcoming flash sheet.

"Hey, you okay?" I ask, surprised to see Sophie again.

"Of course, I just wanted to see you tonight apparently," she says with a shrug, but I don't understand.

"What?" I look at her, confused.

"I was driving home and ended up here. I think my brain subconsciously wanted me to come back over," she says with a blush.

"Oh." I smile. That is incredibly sweet of her, no matter how she thinks she ended up here.

"Is it okay that I'm back?" she asks, and I realize we're still standing in the doorway talking.

"You're always welcome here." I smile and pull her into my arms. She melts into them, and I shut the door behind her with a swift kick.

"So what were you up to the last few hours?" I ask with a chuckle as we make our way to the living room. We take our respective seats on the couch and snuggle together.

"I visited Delilah and her husband and the twins." She smiles. I love the way she lights up when she's talking about babies and kids. I can tell she's going to be an amazing mom someday.

"I'm guessing that was fun...?"

"Well, Delilah slept most of my visit but I had fun with baby Autumn. We bonded and then cleaned up their house for them. I think they needed that more than they wanted to admit. I'll probably be going over there more often to check in on Delilah."

"Is she doing okay?" I ask.

"Yeah, it's just—look don't repeat this okay?"

"Of course, anything you tell me stays between us." I zip my lip and throw away the key for good measure.

"So my brother, Monty. His wife left during a postpartum episode. She decided she couldn't be a mom anymore and fell off the grid. It took Monty months to find her, and then she asked for a divorce. She disappeared without so much as a thought of the girls," Sophie says solemnly.

"Oh, man." I had wondered about the girls' mom but I was never going to ask.

"So I'm just keeping a close eye on Delilah considering she's also the mom to two twin girls. Plus, she's my best friend. I just want to make sure she's not going through anything that I'm not there for her to help."

"That's incredibly kind of you." I reach for her hand.

"I just don't want to miss anything this time. So if I can

help by cleaning up or watching the girls while she takes a nap, I'm there. I just want to help."

"Do you ever think about having kids?" The words slip from my mouth before I can even register what I'm asking. It's not like we're together, and I hope she's not going to take it as me asking her to have kids together.

"I do. I want them, a lot. I'm hoping to have a big family one day," she admits. "Do you think about kids?"

"Honestly? No. I never used to at least, but lately they don't seem to be so bad," I say honestly. Maybe it's the Sophie aspect of it. If I'm going to have babies with someone, I'd want it to be with her. *Whoa, where the hell did that come from?*

No. I know where it came from. Sophie is so caring and compassionate, and I know she'll make one hell of a mother.

"What's with the change?" she asks, and I don't know how to tell her that she's the reason.

"I just think it would be fun to have a little one or two to run after." I smile.

"They're a lot more than you bargain for but I know they're also worth it. I've seen it with Monty, and now I see it with Delilah."

I nod, unsure of what to say next. I'm too busy imagining a life with Sophie no matter how much I keep telling myself it's never going to happen. I see a house with one of those white picket fences and a gaggle of kids running around us. Sophie is happy, pregnant with another, a round belly and a smiling face as she stands on the porch. If I close my eyes for long enough, I can see all of that. I know I'm way too ahead of myself, and my dad's words pop into my head. Maybe I *am* in love with Sophie. But who cares if I am if it doesn't mean anything to her? It's not like I'm going to tell her how I feel.

"Where did you just go? You looked so peaceful." Sophie

traces my chin with her fingers, and I smile. Instead of answering, I lean down and kiss her soft lips.

Our kiss is soft and sweet at first, lingering into a passionate frenzy of touching. My hands are on her chest, and hers are sliding down my neck. I'm moaning lightly into her mouth, and she's nibbling on my bottom lip—it's something new that I'm absolutely in love with.

Her hands linger, running down my chest before pulling my shirt up. She plays with my nipples, and I throw my head back with passion. I love the way she touches me. It's so soft yet so erotic. Sophie dips her head to take my nipple ring in her mouth, and the warm sensation of her mouth has me gasping. I run my hands under the backside of her head and grip on to her hair. I want her to keep going as the pool of heat runs through my thighs and soaks my very thin panties.

"I want you." She whimpers.

"Me too." I nod furiously.

"Go get the strap on," she commands, and I all but jump up. Never has she been so in control during sex, but fuck...it's a complete turn on. She'd gotten in the habit of leaving the strap on here so I grab it from my collection of sex toys in my nightstand and head back to the living room.

"I want to fuck you with it," she says, biting her bottom lip. It's like she's nervous about if I'm going to be into it but when a woman tells you they want to fuck you—a woman who looks like Sophie—you say yes.

"Hell, yes." I nod and watch as Sophie stands before me.

"Sit. I want to strip for you." She smirks and my eyes widen. I'm about to be an incredibly lucky woman.

I murmur an okay and sit on the couch, and she pushes back the coffee table. I watch as she tosses off her T-shirt in one move over her head. Her perky breasts sit on her chest, and her flat stomach is on display. She turns so I can get a view of her dancer's ass, and she slides her leggings down each leg achingly slow. I can feel the heat pooling in my core as she shakes her ass for me. She's wearing a simple pair of cotton white panties but she might as well be wearing a full lingerie outfit for how hot and sexy I find her in this moment. She takes off her bra next, stopping to play with each breast until her nipples are hardened from her touch. I want to reach forward and take them in my mouth, but I keep my hands to myself until I'm instructed not to. It's like a sexy form of torture. Sophie grabs the strap on and somehow pulls it on easily, and as it hangs from her hips, I suck in a breath.

I'm not a fan of giving up control too often, but I do love the sight of Sophie wearing this. She looks like a fucking goddess, and I want to be fucked until I can't walk straight. I spotted her dancer girl tattoo on the side of her hip, and I don't know if it is the fact that I gave her that tattoo or what, but it's hot as hell watching my girl with that tattoo. It's like she was branded by me or something. Do I have a tattoo kink I didn't know about? I don't fuck my clients often. So maybe that has something to do with it.

"I want you naked, but don't touch yourself," Sophie commands, and I nod. I pull off my pajama pants and my panties, sitting on my couch completely naked.

"I want to fuck you from behind, but first I need to make sure you're nice and wet first." Before I can say anything, Sophie drops to her knees. Her tongue darts from her mouth and she spreads my thighs, dipping her tongue in my folds.

"Oh, baby girl!" I scream when her tongue connects with my clit. I was already wet but her tongue working magic on me? Absolute heaven.

"Mmm." I can feel her hum against my folds. She's lapping up all my wetness, and I gasp and moan for her.

"Get on your knees for me," she commands, and I slide off

the couch onto the floor in front of Sophie, lowering my body with my ass in the air.

"I love this tattoo." She comments on the one on my ass. It's a heart on fire, and it says *bite me*. I had it done in my early twenties, and it's one I often forget about.

Except in positions like this.

Sophie leans in closer, and I feel the strap on between my thighs. She's searching for my entrance with her fingers. Once she finds it, she wets her fingers and then coats the strap on completely with my juices. I wasn't worried about taking it, but I am glad she is taking care of me. She slides it in slowly, and I gasp at the pressure. It feels incredible, especially knowing Sophie is on the other end of it. She pushes her hips forward and thrusts inside me.

"Oh, baby girl," I moan again. I love the way she feels inside me.

"You like that, baby?" she says in a sultry voice. It's like she's a sex goddess, and I want to soak up every second of it.

"I love it." I gasp. My breathing is scattered as she starts to move her hips and thrusts her body against me.

"I want you," she whispers. Sophie reaches around and grabs for my breasts. She plays with my nipple ring on one side, and the slight flicks of the metal bar has me gasping at how sensitive my breasts are.

"I w-want you too," I whimper back. She's moving her hips against me, and I'm arching my back to meet her halfway. She moves her hips back and forth, hitting my G-spot with each movement, and I'm calling out in pleasure.

"Oh, baby, tell me how much you want this," she commands and pulls on my hair.

"Oh, fuck!" I scream. "So fucking bad!" I call out. I need a release and fast, I know I'm not going to last between her dirty talk and her touching all over my body. Her hands feel like a flame, and everywhere she touches started a fire.

"Baby, are you close?" she asks with a smirk. I can't see her but I just know she's proud of herself for getting me so close to release.

"Yes, baby girl. I'm so fucking close."

"Then touch your clit and come for me," she says in that sultry tone of hers. Just like that, I'm done.

My hand finds my clit, rubbing fast circles as she pushes in and out of my pussy. I'm moaning and gasping, unable to hold back my orgasm any longer.

"Oh, baby girl! Yes! Yes! Yes! OH yes!!" I scream out, my legs giving out under me as she lets go of my hair and flicks over my nipples one last time. I cry out in absolute pleasure but she doesn't pull out until I'm lying on the ground, panting.

"Fuck," Sophie mutters. "I never thought I'd want to see you lying on the ground looking completely spent, but this does something to me."

"Then get over here and ride my damn face, baby girl," I command. I'm barely over my orgasm but she's looking at me with hooded eyes, and there's nothing I want more in this moment than to eat Sophie's pussy.

Chapter 18

Sophie

Lynn and I are both lying breathless on the floor of her living room. It's thankfully carpeted, although I don't know if my knees would say the same because they definitely have some kind of carpet burn going on. But damn, it was worth it to see Lynn's tattooed ass in my face as she bounced on the strap on like there was no tomorrow.

"I need a snack," I say to Lynn.

"I could go for some cookie dough." She wiggles an eyebrow at me.

"What?"

"I have an idea, but we have to go to the kitchen."

"Okay, but you're carrying me because I'm pretty sure my legs aren't working." I laugh.

"Mine aren't either, think we can crawl?" Lynn and I both glance at the kitchen that can't be more than fifty feet away and laugh.

"If you get up, I'll get up." I compromise with her.

"Okay." She nods.

We both rise together and then laugh at how dramatic it

was for us to do it. Then I follow Lynn into the kitchen where I can see her mind working overtime. She takes out a bottle of chocolate syrup, some whipped cream, and the snowman sugar cookie dough. Are we making some kind of a sundae? I look at the ingredients.

"Lie down on the table," Lynn commands. Sexy and domineering Lynn is back.

"Okay." I lie back, and she surprises me by pouring chocolate syrup over my breasts. One at a time, she makes a small circle of syrup and then begins licking it slowly.

"Oh, fuck." I moan. Her warm tongue melting the cool syrup has me in sensory overload.

"Mmm, you taste so good," she mutters before dripping some over the other breast and doing the same. I close my eyes and let the sensations take over. My thighs are soaked with how wet I am.

I hear the whip cream can next, and Lynn takes it, sprays some down my neck, and then nibbles it off gently. Her teeth graze the skin of my neck with each drop she picks up. It feels incredible. I'm biting my bottom lip, trying to hold back, but then she takes the cookie dough and smears some of it over my belly button. It's freezing cold and the feeling makes my breath hitch. Lynn licks long, and hard over my stomach, her teeth grazing in every spot where the cookie dough resides. She's eating some of it and pouring more chocolate syrup on me, this time in my belly button. It feels like a shot being poured, thankfully I have a deep belly button, and she slurps it up. My pussy is on fire from how turned on I am. It's like she's hitting every turn on spot to tease me completely first.

"God, you're delicious."

"Then taste me." I try to be forceful but the words come out like more of a plead.

"Oh, I love how much you want this." She runs two fingers

Only for the Holidays

up and over my folds. "How much you want *me*," she says with hooded eyes.

"I can't take this." I sit up, pulling her in for a kiss. I want her lips on mine and her body close. She kisses me for a bit as I bite on her bottom lip and take her hands, letting them trail all over my body.

"Lie back," she instructs, and this time she takes the chocolate syrup and pours some in my mouth. She swirls the rich and sticky texture around my mouth with her tongue. The taste of me is still on her tongue from earlier, which causes a frenzy of emotions.

"You're so fucking beautiful," she whispers before pulling away. All I can do to respond is moan lightly.

"I need you to fuck me now."

"All in time, baby girl." She winks and I groan, throwing my head back.

Before I can complain, she's squirting whipped cream over my hip and pubic bones. The cool, light, and airy foam settles into my warm skin. Lynn bends down to take a swipe at my pussy with her tongue before licking over the whipped cream. She hums in appreciation of the taste, and I squirm beneath her touch. She does it again, licking more of the whipped cream this time, and I gasp each time her tongue connects with my clit.

"Oh, fuck," I mumble. I'm dripping all over her face, and she's enjoying every last second of it.

"Here, baby girl." She hands me a piece of cookie dough, and I eat it eagerly. I'm the one who asked for a snack, after all.

"Mmm." She kisses me slowly, tasting the cookie dough on my tongue. I have a feeling this woman is addicted to cookie dough as much as she's addicted to me.

"My two favorite things to eat: you and cookie dough," she says before popping another piece in her mouth.

Instead of teasing me more, she pours chocolate syrup right on my clit, and I gasp as her tongue wastes no time lapping it up. All my juices and wetness cover Lynn's face as she attacks my pussy. Her tongue is working overtime to sop up the chocolate syrup and my juices. She's humming against my pussy, and I'm breathless as she does. My eyes are closed, and all I can see is darkness and feel pleasure. Lynn sucks on my clit, and I cry out.

"Oh, baby!" I scream, and my legs wrap around her head.

She continues sucking on my clit while she puts two fingers inside my pussy and curls them. Hitting my G-spot just perfectly, she follows the sounds of my moans and gasps while I'm thrashing on the table. I'm so turned on to begin with, and everything feels even higher in intensity than usual. I want to come all over her and then kiss it off her lips.

"Baby, I'm so close!" I scream out. She's hooking her fingers, and her tongue is flicking over my clit in overtime.

"I—I'm gunna—" Before I can say it, I feel the intensity of needing to pee, and then I squirt all over Lynn's face. I sit up as best as I can to watch as she holds out her tongue to get every last drop.

"Oh, god, baby girl, that was so fucking hot." She smiles and her eyebrows wiggle as she looks directly in my eyes. But it's too much for me, so I pull her in for a long kiss. Our lips are in a frenzy of control as we both assert our dominance. She eventually wins, but I don't even care, she feels too fucking good being this close to me.

"I want you now," I tell her. I stand, my legs still a little shaky, and then I drop to my knees. I grab the can of whipped cream, squirt some over Lynn's pussy, and then start devouring her.

"Oh!" She screams and grips the counter behind her for support. I've never eaten her out standing up before, but fuck...

it's hot as hell to be on my knees for her. It's like she's in charge, and I just want to please her.

"Baby girl, right there." I squirt more whipped cream on my tongue before diving back between her thighs. The taste of her mixed with the whipped cream is like my own personal sundae. I can eat her out for hours normally, but when she tastes this sweet? It's addicting.

"I need you to fuck me harder," she begs, and I flatten my tongue against her clit.

Before I think twice about it, I crawl to the living room, grab the strap on I'd donned earlier, and put it in my mouth. Lynn's eyes widen as I do, as if I'm giving her a blowjob. It's kind of hot. Then, I slide it inside Lynn, and her eyes roll into the back of her head. My mouth finds her clit, and she's moaning above me. Her hands are in my hair, pulling and pushing my head closer to her body as I'm pushing the strap on in and out of her. She's all but riding the toy while it goes in and out of her pussy. Her hips work overtime to get what she wants from both of us. Pressing my tongue down on her clit, I flick it up and down nice and fast, creating a pattern for her.

"God, just like that!" She screams and cries out for me.

I don't speak, edging her on until she's almost breathless under my touch. Lynn utters a string of curses, her whole body going limp as she comes for me. I don't stop until she pushes my head away, and I slowly pop out the toy from her pussy. She gasps from the loss of it and then stands there, catching her breath.

"Mmm, I love making you come." I stand, running two fingers up her core, and she shivers at my touch. "Sensitive?"

"Yes, so sensitive." She moans lightly.

"Good." I lean in for a kiss, something quick and sharp. She's too weak to handle anything more right now.

"I like the cookie dough, but it's not as fun as the chocolate sauce and whipped cream," she says.

"Yeah, I think I'll still to eating it off a plate," I agree.

"Why don't you go shower off, and I'll make us some real dinner?" she suggests.

"Mmm, I like the sound of that." I nod.

"Need anything? Or you know where everything is?"

"I know where it all is." I laugh. I've been staying here long enough, it isn't my first rodeo.

I grab a towel on the way into the bathroom and then turn the water on. I'm already naked so there's no need to strip down. I step inside and let the hot water warm my body. I wash my hair first, then my body, but it's a lot more fun to shower when Lynn is with me. Deciding not to take too long, I rinse off and head to Lynn's room to find a T-shirt to wear. I love wearing her clothes, they often smell like her, and that makes me feel more calm than I care to admit. It's probably some of those feelings I was trying so hard to push down, but I can't help it. Lynn and I just seem to work. *As friends*, I remind myself. Who knows if we would be able to work as anything else in the future, but all that talk about kids and wanting a big family had to mean something, right? I mean, why would she bring that up if she had no intention of wanting those things with me? It's all so confusing. I should probably just be an adult and tell her how I'm feeling. But not tonight. I need more time to enjoy this and soak up every bit of Lynn I can before I tell her what could be our death sentence.

"Dinner's ready!" Lynn calls just as I'm putting on a fresh pair of panties. I had started keeping a couple of pairs here, which I know sounds like more than a friend thing, but in reality it's just a convenience thing. I'm here so often that keeping panties and a toothbrush around is just good hygiene.

"Coming!" I call back. I run a brush through my hair a few times before tying it in a knot on the top of my head.

When I come out, I see a loaf of garlic bread, a bag of veggies, and a plate full of Alfredo chicken. My jaw drops. Lynn made all of this for me? In the little amount of time I was in the shower?

"Most of it was frozen. Except the chicken, I bought some when you weren't here the other day," she explains.

"It looks delicious." I smile. She's dressed in her pajamas, and her breasts peeking through the thin fabric of her shirt. It makes my mouth water almost as much as this food.

Chapter 19

Sophie

"Look who decided to pick up my call this week," Monty says from the other end.

"Oh come on, we just talked a few days ago."

"That was a week ago, sis," he says sassily.

"Oh, shit."

"Someone's wrapped up with their girlfriend, I see."

"Yeah, something like that." I hate lying to Monty but it's necessary if we're going to keep up the charade.

"I know you're not coming to family dinner tonight, but I thought you might want to come over and see the girls instead this weekend. Maybe Saturday?"

"I'd love to."

"You should bring along Lynn. If you want to."

"Really?" I ask, surprised.

"Yeah, I've seen how you light up around her. It wouldn't be a bad thing for the girls to see what someone in love looks like." He chuckles.

"I'll have to ask her."

Only for the Holidays

"Of course, just let her know she's always welcome with you."

"Thanks, Monty. Everything else going all right? How's the new nanny?"

"She's great. The girls really love her, and she's been so good with them. Mom's still mad about it, but I think it was the best decision for the family."

"Good, you can only do what's best for you," I point out.

"Yeah, I should get back to work but seriously we'd love to see you next weekend."

We say goodbye, and I promise to check with Lynn but either way I'll be there next weekend.

I drive into the back parking lot of Moore Moves and then look at the time. Class will be starting in fifteen minutes, and I didn't even grab a coffee this morning. That's what happens when I stay at Lynn's house and we end up having a quickie before I leave. I'm not complaining though. I can always grab some coffee between classes. I'll never complain about spending more sexy time with Lynn. Or spending time with her in general, honestly. Not that I'm going to admit that to her.

"Hey, Sophie!" Fallon greets me cheerily at the front desk, and I smile.

"Good morning, Fallon."

"Do you need anything? I don't have a class so I'm just doing check-ins today."

"Actually, I would kill for a coffee. Would you mind running over to CRS to grab me one?"

"Of course! Anything else?"

"Nope, I ate a protein bar on the way over, but thank you." I hand her a five dollar bill, and she grabs her jacket before heading next door.

I slip mine off and place it on the hook to my office before I return to the front desk and start checking people in for their classes. It's mostly adults who take my classes—and the occasional college kid.

The attendees greet me as I check everyone in and let them into the studio to stretch. Fallon comes back with my coffee just moments before my class starts, so I grab a hearty sip and then put it in the office to drink after class.

"All right, who's ready to dance?" I say in my perkiest voice. I clap my hands together and lead them in warm-ups. By the time the class is over, everyone has worked up a sweat and is reaching for their water bottles; it's exactly what I want to see.

I stop in the office, look over the notes for my next class while I drink my coffee, and then head back into the studio. It's an adult hip hop class so it's a bit more instructive than the basic dance classes I teach. I toss my coffee in the garbage and start teaching. It's a bit repetitive of a morning, but I love dancing. Especially having such different dances to teach all morning was fun.

I have a break before class number three so I decide to film a few TikTok videos. I set up my phone in the studio and go live for thirty minutes. Then, I look up the latest trending dance, practice it a few times, and then make a few videos. One of them is a quick tutorial of how to do the dance if you're a beginner. I post them, and as I'm scrolling, I see my *likes* pop up as Lynn comments on the video.

LYNN: Wow, you're so talented. 🌀

I SHAKE my head and blush from her comment. I know she was just being honest but it is sweet that she is taking the time out of her day to watch my videos...and comment, too. It's a small gesture that isn't lost on me.

Only for the Holidays

"Soph, your next class is here." Fallon smiles as she knocks on the office door.

"Okay!" I hop up and greet the rest of my class.

I teach and dance and teach and dance until about one o'clock, and then I'm done for the day. It's a short workday, but it's more than enough to pay the bills. We're the only dance studio outside of Portland, so we have a good and loyal clientele base. We charge a decent price for our business, but never overcharge anyone. Delilah and I made a good investment in this place, and I know it was for the best.

I want a shower and a nap after the morning I had. I'm exhausted in a good way. I'm about to head home when I think about Lynn. Am I seeing her again tonight? We hadn't really talked about it, but we have a habit of finding each other at one of our apartments. It's kind of sweet. I don't mind living alone, but I do enjoy knowing I have somewhere to go with someone who wants to see me. It's almost like having someone to come home to. Will that eventually be Lynn?

I don't know why I'm chickening out so hard and not just telling Lynn how I feel. I know I don't have that much to lose but it feels like I have everything to lose. The thought of not being able to be intimate with Lynn anymore is constricting. I know we can only be friends, but I can't help how I feel about her. All I want to do is be with her all the time and see her and spend more and more time just getting to know her. I could live without the sex, but I don't think I could live without the intimacy our *more than friendship* has.

"Bye, Fallon!" I snap myself out of my thoughts on the way out and say goodbye.

I get home in record time and make myself a ham and cheese sandwich, some potato chips, and a smoothie for lunch. I'm hungry and I want to enjoy a nice meal before I take a nap. I put on *Friends* while I eat and watch the mindless TV show.

It's a funny episode, but I'm yawning halfway through, and when I'm done eating, I cuddle up on the couch. It's not as comfortable as when I cuddle with Lynn, but it'll do. I fall asleep thinking about Lynn and how comfortable I am with her—wondering if we could truly ever be more than friends.

***

K*NOCK! Knock! Knock!*

I sit up, startled, and jump up to answer the door. I'm not expecting anyone, but maybe it's Lynn just popping by. Then again, it's still early; wait what time is it? I glance at the clock on the way to the door and realize it's nine o'clock. I slept the entire freaking day away!

"Hello?" I smile groggily, opening the door.

"Thank goodness you're okay!" Lynn gasps and pulls me into a tight hug.

"W-what? Why wouldn't I be?"

"You haven't answered your phone all day. I didn't mean to worry, we don't have to talk 24/7, but I got worried when I hadn't heard anything from you. I sent a text saying I was coming over, and you didn't even say anything," Lynn rambles anxiously. I can't help but smile. Of course she's worried about me. Maybe she does care for me in the ways I care for her after all.

"I'm so sorry. I came home and fell asleep. I was sleeping until you knocked on the door," I explain.

"Oh, well now I feel stupid." She rubs the back of her neck.

"No, it's sweet you were so worried about me." I kiss her lightly on the lips, and she falls into my arms.

"Yeah?"

"Yes, it was very sweet." I press my lips to her forehead and smile.

We shut the front door and Lynn comes in, I realize now that she's holding a bag of Taco Bell.

"Is that Taco Bell?" My eyes widen, and my stomach growls.

"I know it's your thing with Delilah, but I was craving it because I got my period today." She winces.

"Oof, well I'm always down to eat Taco Bell. What did you get?"

"I got you a little bit of everything because I wasn't sure what to get." She walks into the kitchen and puts the oversized bag on the table.

"There's quesadillas, tacos, and burritos." She smiles.

"With cheesy sauce?"

"Of fucking course." She laughs.

"Perfect, I'm down to eat anything then." She starts taking things out of the bag, and I help her pull out the rest. I take a quesadilla and nacho cheese sauce and a burrito to eat and we both veg out on the couch.

"So how was work?" I ask.

"It was okay, I had the worst cramps so I kept taking breaks during tattoos which I never do and kind of hate to do," she explains.

"Having a period sucks. I'm sorry." I reach out and rub her arm gently.

"It does." She sighs.

"Thank you for getting me Taco Bell," I say between bites.

"Well it was before I thought you were missing or something happened to you. It was supposed to be a nice surprise but then I got worried."

"It's still sweet," I insist.

"I can leave after dinner if you want. I know we're obviously not hooking up tonight."

"How about we watch a Christmas movie and cuddle tonight?" I suggest.

"I'd love that." She smiles.

I know it's what we've been doing, but I don't want her to have to leave just because we aren't having sex tonight. I want her to know I still want to spend time with her no matter what we're doing. Especially if it means I can just be held in her arms. But I still don't know how to put that all into words yet. So instead, I stay quiet and ask her to watch Christmas movies with me, and when we cuddle it feels just as amazing as it always does. I sink into her arms, and she kisses my forehead, playing with my hair and rubbing my arm gently. I love the way she touches me aimlessly, like her hands can't be too far from my body at all times. It feels intimate and special—like her body is always connected to mine in some small way.

I think I'm going to tell Lynn how I feel; I just need to talk myself into it. Not talk myself into the feelings, but talk myself into not being so scared. Maybe I'll have a clear head tomorrow and be able to just rip the bandage off. Or at least, that's what I hope will happen. I mean, can I really just carry on like this forever? No. But for now, I watch *the Polar Express* with her, close my eyes, and fall into the ease that is Lynn and me.

Chapter 20

Lynn

I wake up in Sophie's arms and yawn a few times. It's just after ten so I have to get ready for work soon. *Sophie's still here?* Wait, did she skip work for me? My eyes tear up, and I blame my damn hormones for making me so emotional. I'm a wreck and on the verge of telling Sophie how I feel but I keep reminding myself these feelings are temporary, and I don't want to wreck a good thing I have going here.

"Good morning." I kiss Sophie's forehead, and she stirs under me.

"Mmm, morning." She smiles.

"How'd you sleep?" I ask.

"Beautifully." Her eyes are still shut but she smiles fully.

"You didn't have work today?"

"Nah, I called out for once. I wanted to sleep in."

"You're so tired lately, you okay?"

"Someone keeps me up later than I'm used to. Maybe I'm catching up on my sleep," she teases.

I roll my eyes and stretch my arms up, then I move and I feel a gush between my legs. Fuck, what the hell was that? I look down and see blood pooling all over Sophie's pink sheets and through my pants.

"Oh my god, I'm so fucking sorry," I mumble. Full of embarrassment, I jump up and try to clean it up but there's nothing in her room to get it.

"Baby, it's okay." She sits up, looking at it.

"Are you kidding? I ruined your sheets." I frown.

"I've ruined a few pairs of yours." She smirks.

"I'm serious," I say, deadpan.

"So am I. I mean, seriously, it's just a little blood. It'll come out. And if it doesn't, I'll buy new sheets," she says with a shrug. She stands and walks into her bathroom, grabs the Clorox wipes, and before she can wipe it, I stop her.

"Let me get it," I insist. It was bad enough my body made a mess, I wasn't going to have her clean it up.

"Why don't you go take a shower? Or a bath? Run the hot water, use a bath bomb and really relax your body before work," she suggests.

"I don't know."

"How about I bring you some fresh coffee in there, too?"

"You be careful about spoiling me, I might just not want to leave," I tease.

"Good, play hooky with me and stay home too."

"I don't know…"

"You need a sick day. Honestly we should be given sick days for having our periods; our bodies need the break."

"Okay, you've convinced me. I'll text Reagan." I grab my phone from the nightstand and send off a quick text that I don't feel good, and I need the day off. I think I've maybe taken about two sick days in my time of working there, so Reagan checked that I was okay and then said it was no problem.

"Go, bath, now." Sophie points to the bathroom in her bedroom, and I nod.

Only for the Holidays

I strip down, placing my bloody clothes in the sink and turning on the bathtub. Sophie has a variety of bath bombs so I pick one that smells like avocados and dip it in the tub. I lower my body in the tub, and of course either my knees or my boobs are going to be cold but what could I do? Bathtubs weren't made for plus size women. Or women in general, I don't think. It was probably made by some man trying to do the bare minimum to keep his dick clean.

I sigh. The warm water feels amazing on my skin, and after I'm in the tub for a while, Sophie knocks on the door. I pull the curtain over so she can't see the water. Then she comes in with a hot cup of coffee and a donut.

"I forgot I picked these up at the market." She smiles.

"They're perfect." I smile, looking at the powdered donut, and I take a bite with my dry hand. She leans the coffee on the edge of the tub, careful not to spill it.

"How's your bath?"

"It would be better with you in it, but I don't think we'd both fit."

"Hmm, maybe the tub at your place is bigger? Because a bath with you sounds like an amazing time." She smiles.

"I thought so too."

"Speaking of an amazing time, my brother invited me to come over this weekend to see the twins."

"That's great, I know you've been missing them since you've been skipping family dinners." I didn't bring this up but I did notice when she was with me on Sunday nights.

"Yeah, he told me to bring you too." She smiles and my stomach turns.

"Why me?"

"What do you mean?"

"Like as the fake girlfriend thing?" I ask, confused.

"No, like just as..."

"As what?" I prompt.

"I don't know." Sophie goes quiet and bites on her bottom lip.

"I just don't think spending time with your nieces is fair to them when I'm not actually your girlfriend. Parents are one thing, but kids…" My voice trails off.

"I understand." Her mouth forms a tight line.

I don't speak. Suddenly everything feels a little too real for my liking. Like we're suddenly in a committed relationship when we've never even spoken about being together. It feels like it's more serious than I had originally anticipated. I don't know why that's scaring me thought, wasn't this what I had wanted? Does this mean this is what she wants too?

"Tell me what you're thinking," Sophie asks quietly.

This is my moment. It's now or never.

"I like you."

"I like you, too."

"No. I like *like* you," I emphasize.

"I know what you're saying. But I'm trying to tell you the same thing." She giggles, her smile back on her face.

"You do?" My jaw drops.

"I like you, Lynn. Probably since the beginning when I came in for my tattoo. I felt something with you that I've never felt with anyone else before. I want to be with you and not just as my pretend girlfriend, but as my real girlfriend. I want you to be mine so I can shout it from the rooftops and tell everyone I know. I want you to get to know my nieces and my family, as dysfunctional as they are," Sophie says, and my jaw drops even more—if that's possible. It's like everything I was thinking these past few weeks is coming right out of her mouth.

"I like you too, fuck, I think I love you," I say quietly.

"Y-you do?"

"I want all of those things and more, Soph. I want to be

with you and have everyone know it. I want it tattooed on my body even though I don't believe in couple tattoos. Well, matching ones at least. But I do. I really think I love you."

"I-I love you too," she whispers with tears brimming in her eyes.

Suddenly I remember where I am and how I should not be in the tub the first time I'm telling Sophie I love her. I guess it's too late to take it back now. I'm as naked as I feel but I'm also as comfortable as ever because I'm with Sophie. I know I don't have to worry about hiding myself or how I felt with her. I can be myself in every single little way, and I'll be happy.

"Why don't you get in this shower with me so I can kiss you like I want to?" I tell her.

"Yes, please." She nods.

I drain the water quickly and stand up carefully so I don't slip and break anything. Then Sophie, in all her naked glory, steps into the tub. I push her blonde locks out of her face with one hand, and I pull her in for a kiss. But not just any kind of kiss, one of those earth shattering, *I love you* kisses. It's something I've never experienced before a day in my life.

"I love you," I whisper against her lips.

"I love you, too." She smiles and I melt.

Her hands roam my body, desperate for a touch, and I reach for her because I'm just as desperate. I want to be as close to her as I possibly can in this moment. I roam my hands around her neck, running my fingertips down her perky breasts, and take her nipples between my thumb and my finger. She moans in my arms, and I watch her pink pouty lips form a small O as she breathes out in pleasure.

"I want you," I say, breathless. Her body presses against mine, and I reach around her to turn the shower on. It's getting too cold in here without it on. It showers us with cold water first and then changes quickly to hot.

"Fuck me, baby." She whimpers in my arms.
"Yes, baby girl." I nod.

My hands run down the front of her stomach, past her hip bones and straight to her pussy. I play with her clit first, giving it the attention she so desperately wants. Then I run a finger through her folds, and I can feel how wet she is. Her juices cover my fingers, and I bring that finger up to her mouth.

"Clean them," I instruct, and she blushes. She doesn't stop me, instead she leans forward and sucks all the juices off of them.

"Mmm, how do you taste, baby girl?" I smirk.

"I-I taste good," she says with a deep blush. I love knowing I have this sexual power over her sometimes.

I drop my hands back to her pussy, and this time I get a taste. She's right, just as sweet and delicious as usual. Then my hands return to her a pussy for a third time, but this time they don't leave. I press a thumb to her clit, and then I slide inside two fingers.

"You like that, baby? I can feel how much you do," I whisper in her ear.

"I-I love it." She whimpers as I finger her.

Sophies hands are on my ass, gripping tightly and pushing me toward her. We rock against each other, and with the friction and the heat of the shower, it's all too much. I want her to touch me, but instead my free hand falls to my clit. I could get myself off this way without any mess, and I was dying for a release. It was like our first time together all over again.

"I need to touch myself. You're too fucking sexy." I moan.

"That's so hot." She cries.

I'm rubbing fast circles over my clit while fingering her. I pump my fingers in and out of her body until she's screaming my name.

"Oh, baby! Lynn! Oh!" she calls out, and I feel a bit of pressure on my fingers before I'm met with more wetness from her body.

"I love it when you squirt for me, baby girl." I roll my eyes back in pleasure, and with two small circles I can feel my orgasm tightening in my stomach and then I'm seeing stars.

"Oh fuck, fuck, fuck," I mutter, and my orgasm takes over.

"You're so sexy when you come," she whispers against my skin, placing small kisses on my shoulders.

"I love you," I say quietly.

"I love you, too." She smiles like I've just made her day. And if I can, I would do anything to keep that smile on her face forever. Just the look of her as we both wash off is enough to know I made the right decision in telling her how I felt. I couldn't imagine going any longer without her being mine. I'm glad I didn't chicken out or back down at the thought of us and actually let myself find something good for once.

Chapter 21

Sophie

Lynn and I walk to Monty's house holding hands. Lynn even so much as stopped to open the car door for me. She's been nothing but girlfriend material since the day we declared our love for each other. It was completely unexpected that asking to come see my nieces would turn into us admitting our feelings for each other. But hey, whatever works. I'm not going to question why she chose that moment to tell me how she felt. I'm just relived she feels the same way. So we're here to see Monty and play with my nieces, but I'm confused when a blonde I don't recognize opens the door.

"Hi! You must be Sophie, Monty and the girls have told me all about you," she gushes and waves us inside.

"You must be the new nanny," Lynn guesses.

"I am! And you're Sophie's girlfriend, right?"

"Yup," Lynn says proudly.

I'm still shell shocked that *this* was the woman Monty chose to be with his girls. Not that there was anything wrong with her, she's just exceptionally beautiful. She's blonde like me, but she has tan skin and dark eyes. I start to wonder if the blonde is natural or not. This seems like the kind of woman Monty might date, not want to leave alone with his girls.

"I'm so silly. I'm Arabella. It's so nice to meet you both. Monty's on his way home, and he said I can leave when you two get here. Is that okay? Or would you like me to stay?"

"Monty isn't here?" I ask, that's so weird. I thought he was supposed to be here with us.

"He's supposed to be on his way home because a meeting ran longer than expected. He's not too happy since it's a Saturday, and he shouldn't even be working," she says in a hushed tone.

"We're okay to watch the girls." I nod. I'm here and I know how to take care of them. Besides, my brother will be here soon so it's not like this is forever. Lynn looks a little unsure so I squeeze her hand for reassurance.

"Perfect! Girls! Your aunt is here to see you!" Arabella calls for the girls, and they come running in from the living room.

"Hi, Aunt Sophie!" Jesse says excitedly. Jemma stands quietly behind Jesse and pulls on her dress, then she whispers something in her ear and Jesse nods.

"What's happening?" I ask, confused.

"Jemma wants to go play with your girlfriend," Jesse says like it's no big deal. I don't blame her, she has my fearlessness and braveness. But all her sister got was a lot of fear. I worry about her some days because she's not talking as much as Jesse or being as social as other kids her age.

"I'm down to play." Lynn smiles at the girls and then at me.

"Why don't we all play together?" I suggest. I lead them into the living room where the floor is immaculate. I've never seen the bottom of Monty's floor before so I guess hiring this nanny was good for some things.

"I wanna play superheroes!" Jesse exclaims.

"Is that what you wanna play, Jemma?" I ask.

She nods slowly. I don't want to push her to talk if she isn't ready, but I do want to hear my niece's voice again.

"Okay, superheroes it is!" I grab a blanket off the couch and tie it around my neck like a cape. Lynn laughs but follows suit, and so do the girls. Once we all look like superheroes, we pretend to look for signs of trouble. We jump and dance around the room, pretending to fly over the furniture.

"Whoa, what's going on here?" Monty exclaims. We hadn't even heard him walk in.

"We're playing superheroes, Daddy! Be the evil villain we have to defeat!" Jesse says excitedly.

"Okay!" Monty jumps right into character, pretending to have an evil mustache, and tries to steal all the money from the pretend bank the girls set up with Monopoly money.

"Can I have some water?" Lynn asks after we're playing for a bit. It is kind of hot in here.

"Of course." I storm the kitchen, grab each of us a glass of water, and carry the girls sippy cups under my arms.

Everyone drinks and then Jesse pretends the water was poisoned. I don't know how she got to be so creative but it's impressive for someone so young. She tells us all she's going to find the antidote and that she's smart enough not to drink any water. It's quite adorable how she's figuring everything out on her own. Jemma is a perfect sidekick, helping her sister defeat their dad again. Lynn and I are laughing by the time the game is over, and we're all smiling from how much fun we're having.

Playing around like this has me wondering about Lynn and our future. I know we just got together, so I'd never ask these things aloud, but I wonder if our weekends will be filled with playing with my nieces and eventually our own kids. She wasn't shy about bringing this up not too long ago so we're probably on the same page. I can't wait to be pregnant and have a baby with the woman I love. I know it probably won't happen for a while, but I'm excited for all that's yet to come.

"Today was fun," Lynn says as we pile into her car. The girls fell asleep about an hour ago, and we stayed a little later to have some grown up talk with Monty. When he started to yawn, too, we took the hint, and now we're on our way to Lynn's house for the night.

"It was. I'm so glad you came." I smile.

"I am, too. I can't wait to do it again."

I just smile. How lucky am I to have someone who loves me but also my family so much? My heart pings at the thought. Well, not my whole family. I still haven't talked to my mother since Thanksgiving, and Christmas is next week. It'll be the first year I'm not spending it with my whole family. I feel sad about that. It's a tradition that I'll no longer get to be part of.

"Where did you just go?" She glances at me as she drives.

"I don't know." I sigh.

"Baby girl," she whispers, and I'm putty for her.

"I was thinking about my mom and how I won't get to spend Christmas with my family like I usually do." I frown. I didn't mean to bring down the night by bringing this up.

"I'm so sorry. She hasn't tried reaching out to you at all?"

"Nope, not a single call or text."

"I know you knew this was a risk when you brought me around, but are you still sure about us? Because I know how hard it can be to not have family around."

"Stop it. As far as I'm concerned *you're* my family. And Monty and the girls, and Delilah and Ryan and their girls. I don't need anyone in my life who doesn't respect who my partner is." I just wish it didn't have to be this way. I wish my mother wasn't so damn stubborn.

"Well then maybe we should do something special for Christmas."

"Like what?" I look at her, confused.

"Why don't we throw a party? Maybe the day before or the day after. We can invite all our friends who are realistically our family and see them."

"I love that idea." I smile. "But you're not getting out of taking me to your parents for Christmas. If we can't go to mine it means we're spending it with yours."

"You really want to do that?" I ask.

"Of course. Your mother texted me the cutest video the other day about your niece, and now I'm dying to meet her," I admit.

"Oh, gosh." She rolls her eyes but has a smile on her face.

"So your parents for Christmas, friends for Christmas festivities, and then for New Year's we can relax in our PJs eating cookie dough and watching the ball drop."

"Ooo and having sex?" Lynn wiggles her eyebrows.

"Yes. And having sex." I laugh. "That's a given, baby." I blow her a kiss.

"I love you." She laughs.

We make it to her place, and I immediately see Furball. She rubs her body against my legs and purrs at me. Does that mean she's finally accepting me? Does this mean that she likes me? I try not to show too much excitement and scare her away. I bend down to pet her and she lies down, giving me all of her and purring lightly as I rub behind her ears.

"Wow, you two look like you're getting along," Lynn whispers.

"Shh, don't scare her away," I mumble. I shoo her away and

Only for the Holidays

she laughs, heading for the living room. But I don't budge from my spot on the floor. I don't know how long I pet her, but it feels like a long time, and Lynn is grumbling by the time I make it into the bedroom with her.

"It's about time," she teases.

"Sorry, but you know she's never given me undivided attention before. I think she really likes me now," I say excitedly. I strip down into my panties and bra, tossing my bra aside too and look for Lynn's shirt. It's one of my favorites, and she usually leaves it out for me at this point. It's sitting on the bed, so I reach over Lynn and put it on.

"Mmm, do that again," she mumbles.

"Excuse me, there will be no sex tonight," I remind her. One of the things that sucks about having a girlfriend is there are two periods and we haven't quite synced up yet.

"I know, I'm just teasing. Besides, I just love having your body over mine." She bites down on her bottom lip.

"Do you have work in the morning?" I ask.

"Well, at noon." She laughs. "Do you?"

"Yeah, I have to be there at five forty-five," I say with a yawn.

"We better get some sleep then." She folds back the blankets and tucks me into bed.

"Are you working on Friday night?" I ask.

"No, I don't think so. What's up?"

"Can I take you out on a date? We haven't been on an official one yet, and I think I have somewhere I want to take you."

"I'd love to go on a date with you." She smiles.

"Good, then it's a date."

"Where are we going?"

"It's a surprise."

"No, please. I hate surprises." She groans.

"Okay, okay. It's the light show in Portland. I thought we

could go see the holiday lights and then spend the night over there. It can be like a little getaway for the holidays," I suggest. I've been thinking about it a lot this week.

"I'd love that. I'll see if I can take off on Saturday so we don't have to come rushing back for work." She smiles.

"Perfect."

"Maybe we can go to the food trucks that my friend Lainey is always talking about. Carter, from the shop, took her there on one of their first dates and had incredible food. I can't remember what it was, maybe tacos or something, but it sounded good."

"Do food trucks exist in the wintertime?" I ask.

"Oh, hmm, I don't know about that." She pauses. "Well, we can still get something good that we can't find in Seaside. Maybe we can go out for a fancy steak dinner."

"Baby, I'd much rather order room service and have food delivered to our door so I don't have to leave the bedroom with you," I say twirling my hair on my finger.

"Oh, you are too good to be mine. I'm so fucking lucky," Lynn murmurs.

"I'm the lucky one." I smile. She leans in to kiss me softly, and we both fall back into the bed.

Chapter 22

Lynn

"Hey, so have you given any thought to what I asked you?" Reagan asks, tapping on my door.

"I have, and I think I want to do it. But only if we can definitely have the Medusa event."

"Of course! Oh, I'm so excited! You have no idea the favor you're doing me by doing this." She smiles and wraps her arms around me. It's so out of character for both of us but I'm feeling more huggy lately from all the time I've been spending with Sophie.

"I'll draw up the paperwork and have you sign it when you get back on Monday." She smiles. This weekend is my trip to Portland with Sophie. My time off is already approved and Reagan seems happy I'm going away for once.

"Okay, sounds good."

I go back to setting up my tattoo station for my next client. It isn't anything fancy; she just wants some flowers on her shoulder. I set up the chair for that position and get ready to tune out for the next hour or so. The client is nice, but quiet, and she brought along a friend so I doubt she wants to talk to me. But I don't blame her. It's way better to have someone to talk to during these sessions. The ladies gab about people I don't know, and I stay quiet, tattooing away, and when it's all done she smiles like it's the best thing she's ever seen. That's what makes my job so worth it, knowing I'm bringing in so much joy.

She was my last client of the day because I'm leaving early to go see Sophie. She's going to meet me at my apartment so we can drive to Portland together. We don't want to get there too early because the light show starts at dusk, but we want it to be extra dark as we walk around in the lights. So I clock out early, say goodbye to Addison, Carter, and Reagan, and head out for the day.

I'm already packed, so when I get home I put out enough food for two nights for Furball and pray she doesn't eat it all in the first hour. She's usually pretty good about that, though. I don't think I have to worry about her.

"Goodbye, Furball! I'll be back on Sunday night with Sophie." She perks up at Sophie's name, and I love how bonded those two have become lately.

Sophie gets there shortly after so I grab my bag, my coat, and head out for our little adventure. Greeting Sophie with a kiss, I'm happy to say hello to her.

"Hi, baby." She smiles and kisses me back.

"You want to drive?"

"Yup, this is my date. So I'm in charge."

"Oooh! I love a woman who takes command." I wink.

"Hey! Stop that or well never get on the road." She scolds me.

"Okay, okay." I laugh.

"I put the instructions in the car. I made a car playlist but we can't sing too loud otherwise I can't hear the directions."

"You think I'll be singing along to the radio? That's cute but not happening."

"What? That's like road trip goals."

"This is hardly a road trip, we're going like a few hours out of town."

"So we're taking a trip...and we're driving so thus we're on the what? Road. Road trip." She looks at me a matter of factly.

"Okay fine, but I'm still not singing."

"You say that now, but wait until you see what kind of music I've got on this playlist," she teases.

I just laugh and she puts on the playlist and drives away from my apartment. I will admit, the playlist is very catchy. I catch myself tapping my foot and even humming along, but I will not be singing along to any of these songs. I mean, we're two grown adults after all, we don't need to sing like kids. But then Sophie opens her mouth when the Harry Styles song comes on, and I can't help but laugh. Her voice is nothing compared to her dancing; they couldn't be more opposite. But she's laughing and singing along like there's no one here. So I soak up every second of it.

"You should stick to dancing," I tease.

"There's a reason I don't teach singing classes too." She laughs.

"Well, thank you for gracing my ears with that, although I might need earplugs for the ride home."

"What?" She scoffs.

"I love you!" I say quickly.

"I guess I'll need to do some more singing then!" She turns the radio up and on comes another Harry styles song. At least she's singing along to someone I know.

Her voice is nothing like I thought it would be but I just smile and listen as the love of my life sings "Love of my Life." She's belting out all the wrong notes but knows the words perfectly. I'm impressed by how determined she is to sing and how fearless she is in front of me. It's sweet that she doesn't seem to have any inhibitions. I know in this moment...I really do love her. Bad singing and all. It's as if she could do anything and I know I'd love her no matter what.

I've been in love before, sure, I have exes. But I've never loved anyone as strongly as I love Sophie. There's just something different about the way I feel and how strong my desire runs for her. It's like she's in stitched to me. I would be a fool to ever let her and this feeling go. This must have been why my dad had said I loved her; it was probably written all over my face and obvious to everyone but her and I. But I don't care, now that I know and she's mine, I'm going to wear it proudly.

By the time we get to Portland, I'm thankful for the quiet as she looks for somewhere for us to eat. Not that I didn't appreciate her singing, but it was a little much after the third hour. She knows every song on her playlist and loves to belt each one out. It's then that I bring up room service but she reminds me that if we go to the hotel room first, neither of us will want to brave the cold to see the lights. She has a good point. Instead we find a McDonald's to eat while in the car, and then we're headed to the light show.

The sound of Christmas songs blare through the speakers as we shut the car off and walk, hand in gloved hand to the inside of the place. I think it's a zoo during the day but at night they have a variety of lights for the holiday season. Sophie pays for our tickets even though I try to hand her money; she insists it's *her* date. They give us wristbands and then let us into the place. It's absolutely beautiful.

There are Christmas lights in the shape of animals and different scenes. But they also have moving lights where it looks like Santa riding off onto his sleigh with his eight reindeer. The Christmas music in the background is a little distracting but I don't let it bother me. I watch Sophie's face and she's just as mesmerized by the lights as I am.

"We should decorate your house like this," she teases.

"My light bill would be through the roof," I joke.

"Okay, but how about the blaring Christmas music then?"

"I'd never be able to sleep!"

"Good point."

"I think it's nice to see but we shouldn't go doing that to our places."

"True." Sophie's hand is wrapped in mine until she takes my arm and loops hers through, pulling me closer to her. I can smell her vanilla shampoo under her white knit hat, and I instantly feel calm. Something about smelling her scent is enough to relax me. I should look into buying that shampoo and keeping a bottle at the shop for really stressful clients.

"Dance with me!" Sophie exclaims suddenly.

"I don't dance." I shake my head.

"You're dating a dancer, that's like the worst thing I've ever heard."

"Why don't I leave the dancing to you?"

"No, come on." She pushes out her bottom lip to pout at me. Fuck, why is she so adorable? This woman is going to be the death of me.

"People are going to stare," I say quietly.

"Let 'em!" she says with a shrug and holds out a hand for me.

"Fuck it." *If it'll make my girl happy then why the hell not?*

I take her hand, and she squeals with delight. Then the song changes from an upbeat Ariana Grande one to something slow I don't recognize. But Sophie pulls me in close and rests her head on my shoulder. She relaxes in my arms, and I rest my head on top of hers. I love how short she is and how she fits perfectly with me. We slow dance for a while, getting a crowd and some other couples joining us. It's sweet because there are all ages, genders, and races dancing near us and just as in love as we are. It's something amazing to be seen.

"I love you," I whisper against Sophie.

"I love you, too." She looks up at me and smiles. She kisses my lips chastely, not wanting to draw too much attention in the crowd. But then we hear a gasp, and our attention is pulled in the opposite direction.

There's a woman getting down on one knee to ask the woman she's with if she wants to get married. Cheering and gasping roars from the crowd they had accumulated. I couldn't hear exactly what the woman was saying to the other woman, but it must've been good because she was crying the entire time. Then the other woman says *yes,* and the crowd goes wild. Cheers of joy are heard all over. and I smile. I know it's a long way off, but I can't wait to experience something like that with Sophie. And by the look in her eye, I can tell she is thinking the same thing about me. One day we'll have all of those things, and I can tell we'll never be happier.

We continue on with the rest of the light show but nothing compares to the proposal and our impromptu dance. Sophie holds onto me, and we end our way back at the car. Driving to the hotel, we're both exhausted from the day of work and the night we had.

"What do you say to some room service dessert and late night television?" I murmur in the elevator.

"That sounds perfect." She smiles.

"I think I'm too exhausted for anything else," I admit.

"Oh, me too. We can have sex in the morning." She laughs.

We head into the room and after a steamy shower together we calm down for two pieces of chocolate lava cake. It's delivered almost immediately, and we snuggle up in cloth robes in the king sized bed, watching an episode of *Friends*. The cake is more than delicious, and we each finish our pieces. I'm glad I hadn't thought we were going to share one.

"I loved today," Sophie says as she cuddles in my arms.

"I loved today, too. Especially your car singing," I joke.

"Oh shush, I know you actually loved it."

"I actually did. I think I love everything about you."

"Well, I could do without your sass," she teases.

"Me? Sassy? Never." I fake gasp.

"Alright, get some sleep. We have a big day of nothing to do tomorrow, and I plan to do it all day long." She yawns.

"Sounds perfect to me."

Chapter 23

Sophie

After our weekend together, the last thing I want to do is get up early and go back to work. But there's only three more days until Christmas, and I need to get through these classes. Only half of the people in my classes show up, and I don't blame them. The weather is shitty, and it's even colder because it's so early. I didn't mind it so much until I started dating my night owl girlfriend. I hate being on opposite schedules from her, but we still manage to make it work.

I'm just about done with classes when Fallon calls me to the front.

"What's going on?" I ask with a smile. I hope it isn't a rude customer I'll have to deal with this close to Christmas.

"Your, um, mother…is here I think," she says, unsure. Sure enough, just five short feet away, my mother is standing in the corner looking over the wall of holiday cards we've received from clients this year. I walk over and stand next to her, my shoulders square and ready for whatever I have in store.

"What's going on?"

"Can't you say hello first?"

Only for the Holidays

"I'm sorry, Mother, hello, good to see you. Now, why are you here at my place of work?"

"I want to discuss something with you." She exhales sharply.

"Come to my office." Delilah isn't here yet so I'll be able to have a private conversation without anyone overhearing. My mom follows me to the back, and I don't offer her a seat, but instead fold my arms after closing the door behind us.

"What?" I repeat. I wanted to get this over with as quickly as possible.

"I want to apologize for what happened on Thanksgiving."

"You mean when you basically kicked my girlfriend out and then said some incredibly rude and homophobic things?" I've never been this blunt with my mom, but I'm tired of being afraid of her.

"Yes, for that." She's clearly uncomfortable, so I'm not entirely sure why she's here. I can't tell if this apology is genuine or just for show.

"Did Dad or Monty put you up to this?"

"No. They did recommend I mend fences, but they don't have any idea I'm here. I'm here on my own," she says proudly.

"Okay." I'm a little bit impressed but I'm not going to let her know that.

"I was just so surprised to see you with someone like *that*. With a woman, no less. I thought you were just trying to get a rise out of me like when you were a teenager." I bite my bottom lip. She does have a point.

"I understand that. But what Lynn and I have is real."

"You really want to be with a woman? Like get married and all of that?"

"Yes. She makes me incredibly happy. Happier than any man has in the past," I explain.

"Okay. Then I guess I will need to get used to that," she says with a tight-lipped smile.

"Really?"

"I won't lie and say that I'm happy about it. But if she treats you right and makes you so happy then I should at least give her a chance. I can't help that she's a woman, and that's who you want to be with. I'll work on accepting it. But you have to give me some time." I can tell she's been struggling with this. But as much as I want to tell her it's not enough, it is. She's willing to try because she sees that Lynn makes me happy, and that's all I can really ask for from her.

"Okay. I can do that." I nod.

"Really?" She's the surprised one now.

"I just want you to accept me for who I am. It's all Monty and I have ever wanted. We aren't going to be like you, but that doesn't mean we don't love you."

"I know. It's just hard raising two children that are so independent. I don't know how that happened," she says wiping her eyes.

"Because you did such a good job raising us." I smile and lean in for a hug. She tightens her grip around me and pulls me in even closer.

"I'd love for you and Lynn to come for Christmas. It wouldn't be the same without you."

"We would love to, but we have plans with her family. Maybe we could come for Christmas Eve?"

My mother bites her tongue. I can tell this is going to be a give and take for both of us. "Okay, that would be okay." She nods. I know Christmas is her favorite holiday, and it'll be weird not going there for once, but then again, I don't want to bail on Lynn's family either. My mom will have to be okay with me not dropping everything to do what she thinks is best.

Only for the Holidays

"I better get going, I have some shopping to do." She smiles and takes her purse before leaving.

"Bye Mom, I love you," I call after her.

"I love you, too." She smiles and I swear it's genuine.

♡♡♡

I'M TELLING Lynn all about my mom when I get to her place tonight. She's not home yet, but she told me where she keeps the spare key, and I let myself in. It's weird being in her house when she's not home, but it's a nice sort of next step for us. We trust each other to hang out in each other's places when the other isn't home. I play with Furball and call Lynn on the phone while she drives home from work.

"I'm so happy for you, baby girl. I know it was really eating away at you not being able to see your mom for the holidays. If you need to go there for Christmas instead of Christmas Eve, I understand that too."

"No, I want to get to know your family better, and I can only do that if I go," I insist.

"Okay, but only if you're sure."

"I am, definitely."

"I'll be home in exactly one minute, I'll see you soon, baby girl." She hangs up, and I look at Furball. Why hadn't she named her cat something a little bit nicer? Furball is such an odd name, but it's also kind of fitting once you get to know her. I wonder if she wants more pets down the line or it's just Furball forever. I'm contemplating how a kid and Furball would get along when I hear the front door unlock.

I run toward Lynn with my arms open and crash into her.

"I love you," I murmur against her neck.

"I love you, too."

"I missed you," I add.

"I missed you, too," she says with a light chuckle.

She's holding bags full of groceries, and it's starting to snow again so I grab them from her. Well, some of them. She's carrying all thirty bags at once so she doesn't have to make a second trip, and as much as I respect that, I couldn't do it. My dainty arms are just not made for holding that many grocery bags at once.

"I thought I'd make us dinner; I'm a little tired of takeout," she explains as we place the bags on the counter and begin unloading them into the fridge.

"I'd love that. What are you making?"

"How do you feel about chicken stir fry?"

"Sounds delicious."

"Perfect, it's one of my favorites to make because it's so simple."

I take a seat at the table and watch as Lynn starts preparing the dinner. It's so cute watching her put everything together. It's like I'm on my own personal cooking show. The only thing that could make it better is if she was cooking naked. But I don't know how safe that actually is. I don't want her hurting herself—especially while cooking. I nix the naked part of my daydream and watch as she prepares the dinner.

Part of me starts to wonder what it might be like to live with Lynn. I guess we basically are already but there's still a security in being able to go back to our own places if we want to. Plus, we have very different vibes. I'm more pinks and light colors while she's a darker black vibe. What if we try living together and it doesn't work out? What'll happen to us? Another thought pops into my head...what if it actually works out? What if we move in together and it's as perfect as things are now?

"Did I lose you?" Lynn asks with a chuckle.

"What?"

"I asked if you wanted anything to drink." She laughs.

"Oh, just water please." I smile.

"It'll be ready in about six minutes," she says proudly.

"Perfect." I nod.

"What were you thinking about so deep in thought?"

"Honestly?" I ask, chewing on my bottom lip.

"Yeah, if you feel comfortable sharing."

"I was thinking about how things might work if we lived together. If they'd be as nice as this is," I admit with a blush.

"Oh..." She pauses. "I think they'd be as nice as this."

"But?" I can sense a hesitation in her voice.

"I'm not quite ready for that step yet," she admits.

"Me either! I was just daydreaming! I promise!" I exclaim, and she looks relieved.

"One day," she murmurs, and I nod.

"Okay, dinner is almost ready, plate or bowl?"

"Um, bowl?" I feel like it's a trick question but it is more fun to eat things out of a bowl.

She pulls down a bowl for me and a plate for her. Even with the little things we are quite opposite. But we still manage to work.

"So, I told Reagan I'll take the promotion at work." She smiles.

"Holy shit, that's awesome!"

"I told her I want to do something big for the Medusa event, and she gave me free reign to plan it. I'm going to come up with a solid plan before I bother everyone about it." She sets down the plate and bowl at the table and brings two glasses of water over. She sits across from me, and we talk and eat.

"I can help. I know you need tattoo artists but I can drum up some business from TikTok. Maybe create a dance called *the medusa* to make it go viral or something?" I'm just spit balling ideas, but Lynn looks super impressed.

"Yes, please. I want this to be something big that helps a lot of people. I think it'll be the one time the shop charges for Medusa tattoos, and all the benefits will go to RAINN."

"That would be amazing, you could have people come in and do one of those sheet things that I've seen you guys do for holidays."

"You mean a flash sheet?"

"Yes! One of those."

"Hmm, maybe they could all be Greek goddesses that me and the other artists could tattoo to keep with the theme."

"That would be so cool." I nod.

"I'm sure the other girls would want to be in on it, I'll have to check, of course, but I think this event could be huge. And it'll create business and attention for the shop in general which could be a great thing."

"I could see this being a great thing for you, baby. I'm so glad you decided to go for it." I smile.

"Well I couldn't have done it without you. I really only said yes because you convinced me I could." She reaches for my hand and holds mine in hers for just a moment.

I smile. I feel an ease around Lynn that never seems to go away—no matter how much I worry it might disappear. I know we're still in the honeymoon phase, but it doesn't feel like that. It feels like more than that, like Lynn is my person, and I'm deeply connected to her. There's an ease about the two of us being together and working out no matter what. Like all my fears vanish when she's around.

And even though this was supposed to be only for the holidays...I think what the two of us have is less about a moment in time and more about forever.

BONUS EPILOGUE
Lynn

Today's the day I've been waiting for, the day that I've been planning for months. Well, with the help of Sophie of course. Today is the day the shop opens for the Medusa Event, as Sophie and I have been calling it. Addison, Carter, Reagan and I have all gotten together to create a flash sheet of tattoos that represents each of our styles. Mine was more edgy while Addison's was softer and Reagan and Carter both had a mix to theirs. It was going to be paid tattoos for $75 each with all the proceeds going toward RAINN. We would also be scheduling anyone who wants to get a Medusa tattoo for free from me in the future. It was the perfect way to raise awareness while also making money for the cause.

Sophie had brought in Delilah and Fallon to help be receptionists for the day. They would be taking payments, manning the phones and setting up for tattoos so it could be a quicker turnaround.

I was currently resting my hand in one of the hand massagers Sophie had gotten me for Christmas. I knew today was going to be a crazy hectic day and I didn't want to have to tap out early because of my hand cramping. I wanted to be hanging signs and doing more to help but Sophie had insisted I sit and relax, at least for now.

"I think the banner is a little low." Sophie says standing back. Delilah and Grayson are hanging it since they're our two tallest people. The guys were here to hold the door, offer water and help in any ways they could but they knew they weren't the stars of the show. And honestly, they weren't trying to be. I think Grayson and Ryan were just happy to have a day off from their kids.

"It looks good babe, no one is going to hit their head and that's the main concern." I remind her.

"Okay, you're right." She nods and gives them the thumbs up to tack it to the wall.

"Is everything ready to go?" I ask.

We had printed out a ton of stencil sheets and prepped them in one of the spare rooms so we could easily grab them for whatever tattoo the person wanted. It helped that they were only offered in one size. It made it easier on us for sure.

"Water in all the rooms?" Sophie starts reading off a list she created to Delilah and Fallon.

"Check." Fallon nods.

"Ink set ups ready?" She looks at me.

"All good to go." We were keeping the tattoos to red, black, and white to keep things simple too.

It was rare we did flash sheet sales, except for Friday the 13th, but that only came around every so often. So we didn't have a system down yet but we were on our way, especially with Sophie's organization. I stand from where I'm sitting with the hand massager and call out for Reagan to take a turn. I knew she'd need to relax just as much as I did. She had just as much riding on today as I did.

"I'm here!" She calls from the back and promptly sits down and puts her hand in the massager.

"I need to see you in the back for a minute to go over supplies." Sophie instructs me.

"Okay." I nod. I didn't know what we needed to go over but she had mapped out this place entirely. So I knew she was on top of everything.

"What do we need to—" I'm immediately ambushed by the door closing behind me and Sophie's lips clinging to mine.

"Mmm," I hum against her.

Pulling back, I look at her. "What's going on?"

"I just wanted you to remember to relax, and I figured this was the best way to do it." She says with a smile.

"Oh, well if it's what the doctor ordered." I wink and lean back in to kiss her. Our tongues sliding into each others mouths and our bodies pushing against the door. We kiss and lose ourselves in this moment together.

Until there's a knock at the door.

"Sorry to um interrupt but there's a line forming and it's time to open the doors." Fallon calls from the other side of the door.

"Okay!" Sophie calls out and I see a blush creep over her cheeks from being caught.

She straightens out her sweater with Aphrodite on it and I fix my t-shirt that was complete with a drawing of Medusa on it. We were sticking with the Greek Goddesses vibes today. It was only fitting that the woman I loved had the Greek Goddess of Love.

"You two weren't you know... in there were you?" Fallon asks surprised.

"No, we were just kissing." I say with a shrug and Sophie hits my shoulder. "Ow."

"Anyway, you said there was a line?" Sophie asks changing the subject.

"Oh yes, come see." Fallon brings us back to the front of the shop where the front space was already crowded with people but what was most impressive was the line forming outside. The guys were doing crowd control but there was at least 100 people out there already and we hadn't even opened officially yet.

"Holy shit." I mumble.

"I guess this is what happens when you put out ads and share on TikTok." Sophie smiles proudly. "Now go do your thing!" She shoves me toward my office and Fallon brings in the first woman to be tattooed by me.

"Hi, I'm Lynn." I introduce myself and the day begins.

Customer after customer, we're in for a long ass day. I don't have a second to breathe, except for the twenty minutes of lunch Sophie insists I have with a full bottle of water. If she wasn't taking care of me I don't know what I would do.

"Are you ready for more baby? We've had a few people insist on waiting for your flash sheet specifically."

"You did?" I can't help but smile.

"Of course, you're incredibly talented. Not that the other girls aren't, but you know I'm biased." She shrugs.

"Well yes, bring them in." I nod.

"I need two more in here!" Sophie calls out and in comes two guys looking for a design from my flash sheet. They surprise me by showing me their Medusa tattoos first.

"We know you didn't do them, but we think it's incredible that you do them so often. And for free to those survivors who can't afford it." One of them says.

"We are both survivors, actually meeting in a survivors club of sorts. So it's incredible that you put together this event." The other one says.

"I'm also a survivor, so it was super important to me because I know how much getting this tattoo felt like I was getting a part of control of my body back." I explain showing them my shoulder.

"We felt the same. We're going to be making the drive anytime we want a tattoo from now on. We'd like you to be our official tattoo artist." He says smiling.

"I have to ask your names then, and where are you guys from?"

"Portland, so not too far." He says. "I'm Matt." He adds.

"I'm Justin." The other one smiles.

"Well, let's get started before my girlfriend complains I haven't tattooed anyone yet and you can tell me more about you guys."

They chuckle and Justin hops up first, holding hands with Matt as I tattoo a skull with roses on his wrist. Then Matt hops up and I do a heart on fire on his arm.

"I love it, please take a picture and we'll be sure to share it everywhere." They ask. So I take a bunch of photos and they sharpen the image to show off the tattoo and post it right away, tagging my instagram too.

"It was great meeting you both. I'll look forward to seeing your names on my books." I smile.

"Definitely." Justin and Matt leave and not a second later, Sophie comes in and gasps. All wide eyed, she's making faces and smiling at me.

"What? You're creeping me out." I laugh.

"Do you know who that was?"

"Ummm Matt and Justin?" I look at her confused.

"They're famous YouTubers! They have a TikTok account where they talk about their experiences and help other survivors. They are amazing exposure for what you do baby." She says proudly.

"Wow, that's amazing." I had no idea.

Fallon and Delilah come running in a few minutes later. "We have to tell you this right now!"

"What?" We look at them wearily.

"Those guys just left an anonymous check for twenty thousand dollars!" They exclaim and push the check toward Sophie and I.

"What?!" We both exclaim.

"Holy shit." I say taking a better look.

"They wanted it to be anonymous and just as a thank you for all you're doing. How crazy is that?" Delilah explains.

"My goal was only 5k for the event." I say quietly.

"Baby, you just quadrupled your goal and it's barely noon." Sophie says proudly grabbing my face and kissing me softly.

"Holy shit." I say again.

"Wow."

"Well, there's more people to tattoo or we can stop the event early, it's up to you." Sophie says.

"No, we tattoo everyone. We raise as much money as we possibly can for RAINN and then we can call it a day." I say to everyone. They nod and smile, this was just the beginning of today.

Sophie calls in the next client and I tattoo them happily. Client after client, I don't care about the money, I'm just happy to be doing my job. There's nothing like being able to bring joy to people in such a permanent way. I make sure everyone is happy by the time they're leaving and although my hand is cramping, I ask for the next customer.

The name sounds familiar but what surprises me is how familiar she looks. Then I remember, she's the one I tattooed a Medusa on just a few months ago.

"Kate," I say suddenly remembering her name.

"You remembered me?" She says happily.

"I'm glad you're back."

"I saw this event and knew I needed to come. I got a new job and I'm making money again and I can pay for this one. So when I saw the money was going to RAINN, I knew I couldn't pass up the opportunity." She explains.

"I'm so happy for you." I smile.

Grabbing the stencil, I place the small heart on fire on her left forearm where she wants it and then I begin tattooing. She's just as calm as last time and I remember she was fairly easy to tattoo. If I remember correctly, she was one of my tattoos on the day I met Sophie. Or very close to that day.

"I hope you continue to come back, I'd love to see you again." I tell her when her tattoo is done.

"Thank you. I most definitely will." She smiles.

Sophie makes me take another break which consists of putting my hand in the hand massager and drinking another bottle of water. Considering I hadn't peed much today, I was probably dehydrated from all the work I was doing. So I didn't protest as she fed me water.

"You only have five more clients and then we're done for the day. We closed off the line and gave everyone a discount card to come back another day just like you said."

"Perfect, I'm a little tired." I admit.

"Of course you are you've been tattooing like a maniac." She laughs.

"Well, it'll all be worth it." I decide.

I tattoo four more people and then Sophie hops up on the sterile table. Now I was going to have to clean it again for person number five, but I don't complain at her. She was just being cute. And I loved seeing her in my chair for once. It reminded me of how we met.

"Where's number 5?" I ask confused.

"You're looking at her. I'd like a tattoo please." She smiles.

"Really?"

"Of course, what a better way to commemorate the occasion." She smiles proudly. "This way we'll always have a reminder of today."

"I love that." I kiss her lips softly and then start setting up. "What will it be, babygirl?"

"I was hoping for that special one, I didn't see anyone pick it today."

"You mean the Medusa heart?" I ask. She was right, I hadn't had a chance to tattoo any of them today and she knew it was one of my favorites to draw.

"Yes please. I know I don't have the same experience as you with Medusa, but I love the design and it makes me feel connected to you. Is that okay?"

"Of course it is my love, you don't have to explain yourself to me."

The heart was atomically drawn but instead of the valves at the top, there were snakes coming out of it. I loved the way the drawing came out and I would love seeing it on Sophie's body even more. Her art on my body was such a fucking turn on, I definitely had a kink for that. Whether that be branding her or just knowing it's my art, I didn't care. She was mine and I wanted everyone to know it.

Of course, little did she know I was planning on proposing sometime soon. I had the ring in my drawer at home and I was just looking to figure out the perfect time and place for us. I wanted it to be somewhere that represented us while also being somewhere she loved. I still needed to think on it, but I was sure about one thing. Sophie was going to be my wife one day and that was all thanks to a little while lie I told my mother and father. If I had never asked her to be my fake girlfriend, I sometimes wonder if we would've still ended up here. Sophie insists

Only for the Holidays

that we would, that our souls are interconnected in some way that was inexplainable to anyone else.

"How do you like it?" I ask when I'm all done.

"Oh my gosh it looks so cool! I love it!" She smiles genuinely at it and I'm relieved. There was nothing scarier then tattooing your girlfriend and worrying she might not like it.

Sophie kisses me lightly and I'm relieved that she likes it. Then we gather the rest of the group as Fallon and Delilah finish counting up the total for the day. I had told them to keep the big donation a secret until we tallied up the total. So when they hand me the total, even I'm shocked by how much money we made today.

"I want to thank everyone for donating their time and effort today. I know it was a long and grueling day on our hands especially, but it shows how much we can give back to those who desperately need it. We raised over thirty-one thousand dollars today." There are gasps and applause from everyone in the room. "So it's something Reagan and I might be doing more than once a year moving forward, but we really appreciate all you guys did for us today. Especially thank you to Sophie, who without her, this event never would have happened."

"And thank you to Lynn, who is being super modest, but without her idea this never would've come to fruit." Sophie adds.

Everyone claps for us and I'm so thankful for the day I've had and how much I'm glad to be apart of this little tattooing family.

Acknowledgments

Thank you to everyone who has been with me since the beginning with *Only for the Summer*. This series was originally, *Only in Seaside* with a mix of MF and FF romances, due to marketing choices it's now been split into two different series. Making this the book in the *Seasons of Seaside* series. I don't want to call it the last book, because although, for now it is, I might be tempted to come back to Seaside in the future.

Thank you to my grandma for always believing in me and helping me in so many ways. Thank you for watching Teddy so I could actually write this book. Thank you for being one of my biggest supporters.

Thank you to my sprinting buddies; S.E. Green and J.J. Grice. I don't know what I'd do without you both cheering me on and kicking my butt into gear.

Thank you to all the readers who picked up Only for the Summer and Only for Convenience and convinced me to continue writing this series. I'm so glad to give you a glimpse into Seaside.

Thank you to Teddy for being my little cheerleader and telling anyone who will listen that his mommy writes books. I love that you are so proud of me, you're one of the biggest reasons I'm doing this.

Thank you to my ARC and Beta readers for helping read and review all my books, the many many drafts and telling me what is and isn't working.

I'm not done with Seaside yet, meaning my next series *Sweet in Seaside* will be coming out in 2024! 4 brand new books with Brand new characters, all the same romance, and steamy as hell. I can't wait to bring you on a new journey with me!

Preorder Sweet on You HERE

Also by Shannon O'Connor

SEASONS OF SEASIDE SERIES

(each book can be read as a standalone)

Only for the Summer

Only for Convenience

Only for the Holidays

Only to Save You

SWEET IN SEASIDE SERIES

(each book can be read as a standalone)

Sweet on You

Sweet as Honey

Sprinkled with Love

Semisweet for You

ETERNAL PORT VALLEY SERIES

Unexpected Departure

Unexpected Days

STANDALONES

Electric Love

Butterflies in Paris

All's Fair in Love & Vegas

Fumbling into You

Doll Face

Poolside Love

A Shot at Love

THE HOLIDAYS WITH YOU

(each book can be read as a standalone)

I Saw Mommy Kissing the Nanny

Lucky to be Yours

The Only Reason

Ugly Sweater Christmas

POETRY

For Always

Holding on to Nothing

Say it Everyday

Midnights in a Mustang

Five More Minutes

When Lust Was Enough

Isolation

All of Me

Lost Moments

Cosmic

Also by S O'Connor

ONLY IN SEASIDE SERIES
(each book can be read as a standalone)

Only for Revenge

Only for the Baby

Only the Beginning

ETERNAL PLAYERS SERIES

The Accidental Puck

Also by Shannon Renee

MORE LOVE SERIES
Something Like Us
When it Comes to Us (Coming soon)
Stay Here With Me (Coming soon)

About the Author

Shannon O'Connor is a twenty-something, bisexual, self-published poet of several books and counting. She released her first novel, *Electric Love* in 2021 and is currently working on a sapphic romance novel set for summer 2022. She is often found in coffee shops, probably writing about someone she shouldn't be. She sometimes writes as S O'Connor for MF romances and as Shannon Renee for Poly romances.

Heat. Heart. & HEA's.

Check out more work & updates on:
Facebook Group: https://www.facebook.com/groups/shanssquad

Website: https://shanoconnor.com

Printed in Great Britain
by Amazon

32448108R00101